HARLEQUIN ROMANCE®

3359
$2.99 U.S.
$3.50 CAN.

FAITH, HOPE AND MARRIAGE

Emma Goldrick

"Harry," he suggested again. "My name is Harry. I'd appreciate it if you'd call me Harry."

"Harry. I'll call you Harry." Faith gave in.

"Why did you give in so easily?" Harry asked.

"Give in?" Faith questioned.

"Yes. Give in. As in concluding that you could safely use my first name. Or do you believe that we won't be seeing each other again?"

"I don't see why I should see you again," Faith said, just a little upset that he could read her so easily.

"We will be seeing each other again," Harry said with conviction.

"Why?"

"Because St. Kitts is a very small island. And Lady Sunny is a dedicated matchmaker."

"Why," Faith asked, "do you feel that Lady Sunny will be bringing us together in the future?"

"Just call it instinct."

Dear Reader,

I am honored to have one of my books featured in
Harlequin Romance. I've turned to Faith Latimore,
the lawyer-daughter of Mary Kate and Bruce Latimore,
who found the law not quite to her taste. After all,
her sister Becky had married a doctor after a wild
adventure, her sister Mattie went to Africa and had
been bought for a significant bride price, and all Faith
could find for herself was a job as companion for an
earl's elderly daughter. So, read Faith's story as she, too,
dares to dream....

Emma Goldrick

FAITH, HOPE AND MARRIAGE
Emma Goldrick

Harlequin Books

TORONTO • NEW YORK • LONDON
AMSTERDAM • PARIS • SYDNEY • HAMBURG
STOCKHOLM • ATHENS • TOKYO • MILAN
MADRID • WARSAW • BUDAPEST • AUCKLAND

To Jacqueline Helen Hayward, for all her help
and good cheer—Jackie, this is all of it

ISBN 0-373-03359-1

FAITH, HOPE AND MARRIAGE

Copyright © 1995 by Emma Goldrick.

First North American Publication 1995.

Printed in U.S.A.

CHAPTER ONE

'IT's the name that intrigues me.' Faith Latimore squirmed in her chair and studied the eagle face of Eli Whitmore—of Whitmore, Whitmore and Bledsoe, Gray's Inn, London. 'Lady Sunny?'

'Lady Griselda,' the old lawyer conceded. 'She was called Lady Sunny at her come-out, back between the wars. Because of her disposition, you know. The name has stuck. Everyone uses it, including herself.'

'And my job would be to——?'

'To go to her villa in the Caribbean—St Kitts, to be exact.'

'And?'

And then the smile. As if he had steel teeth, and all of them hurt. 'Lady Sunny still thinks she is young, my dear. She is busier than, as you Yankees say, a one-armed paper hanger. She needs someone—a companion—to serve as her legs, so to speak.'

'And there's nobody on St Kitts who could——?'

'Perhaps I should be more direct, Miss Latimore. In the past six years we have sent five different companions to Lady Sunny. All of them ended up by marrying. Now you, in your submission, indicate that you have no interest in marriage?'

Faith took a deep breath and shuddered at the dark remembrances. Elison Fane, back in Massachusetts. He had been interested in her position in Latimore, Incorporated, the third largest construction firm in the United States, and had managed to hide that interest until three days before the wedding. She'd fled to England

and met Sir Harry Watson—a delightfully bluff
Yorkshireman, who had needed a wife to secure his own
inheritance, and had pursued her until she'd found he
was an alcoholic!

I'm just not a good judge of men, she told herself as
she looked up to find Eli Whitmore staring at her. She
nibbled on her lip. 'No,' she said firmly, 'I have no
interest in marriage.'

'Well, that certainly will be helpful,' the lawyer commented. 'Now, here is what you must do.'

Within the hour Faith Latimore was sitting all alone in
a chartered jet, hardly crowded by her meager wardrobe,
her law degree from Harvard, her Ph.D. from Oxford.
She carried ten thousand questions, none of which was
answered before the plane took off. But there was a loose-
leaf book waiting for her in the aircraft. By the time she
landed at Golden Rock Airport on St Christopher Island,
and was installed as the *domina*—the manager—of the
sprawling, reinforced concrete villa which marched up
and down the side of Old Stone Fort Hill, higgledy-
piggledy, like a design accident of major proportions,
she thought she knew quite a bit. Perhaps not all of it
was true.

Rose Cottage. 'Cottage', like those fifty-room stone
'cottages' in Newport, Rhode Island.

'Fifty-six rooms,' Napoleon assured her.

'But you must surely see,' she insisted to Napoleon,
the butler from Montserrat, whose lilting speech, with
a touch of the Irish, rolled over her like a distant fog,
'I have to see Lady Sunny. There are decisions to be
taken.'

'But you have only been here five days,' that worthy
insisted. 'Hardly a minute in time. Lady Sunny tends to
think of such actions as hasty! Precipitate, actually.'

'Well, hasty or no, I intend to be seen. Where is she?'

The butler waved vaguely in the direction of the huge porch that circled the villa. 'On the veranda. But I wouldn't, *domina*.'

But Faith Latimore would. 'And that's another thing,' she said firmly. '*Domina*. It sounds like royalty. I would prefer to be called Faith.'

The butler blinked at her. 'You are, of course, in charge of most things in the cottage,' he said. 'We could compromise. All the underservants could call you Miss Faith?'

'Faith,' she insisted.

'Miss Faith,' he returned. 'I, of course, will continue to call you *domina*.'

Faith gave up the lost cause and started to hunt Lady Sunny.

The beige wooden porch wandered as much as the rest of the building, almost as if it had been designed in paper and then stapled on to the house, leaning over the edge of the cliff. Faith passed through more rooms than she could count, then was expelled on to the veranda, more by force of the tropical breeze than anything else. The broad stretch of veranda which hung out over the edge of the hill was almost empty. In one corner a smiling maid stood. In the middle of the open area a large pouffe was the center of six ambitious little black kittens. And on the pouffe itself a tiny, rotund, white-haired lady sat— a woman who reminded Faith of pictures of Queen Victoria in her latter days. She wore a huge smile on her soft, rounded white face as she played with the kittens. She looked up as Faith came in sight.

'Ah. I was expecting you. Not necessarily today, of course, *domina*.' A little giggle accompanied the statement.

Lady Sunny, Faith told herself.

The little lady patted the edge of the pouffe in invitation. She was wearing a long black dress that reached to her ankles, and a bright string of pearls which filled the gap at her square-cut neck. 'My, you are certainly a big young lady.'

'Five feet ten,' Faith returned. 'My father is a very big man, although my mother is rather—small.'

'Mine too,' Lady Sunny returned. 'But *we* all turned out to be tiny creatures. There were seven of us, you know.' She nodded sagely, as if the world knew. 'Seven daughters. My father was somewhat disappointed. The earldom, you know. It passed out of the family at his demise. Some Canadian fellow or other inherited. But Father, despite his disappointment, treated us all with love, made a special effort to marry us off happily, and was altogether a delightful father. And yours?'

'A fine man,' Faith admitted. 'Although, to be honest about it, my mother rules the family.'

A tiny grimace ran across the lady's face. 'How unusual,' she murmured. 'My father ruled the roost. But earls had a tendency to do that in my day. And Dicky——'

Faith came to the edge of the pouffe and coiled herself up on the floor, putting them both at conversation level. 'Dicky? Your husband was of the aristocracy?'

'Better than that,' Lady Sunny giggled. 'Dicky was in shoes. Factories all over the world. Look.' She displayed a pair of light blue slippers, sparkling with diamanté inserts at the toes. 'From my factory in Singapore—or is it Hong Kong? Or Luanda?' She shrugged, and her whole body shrugged with her. 'Not important. But my favorite color. You have lovely hair.'

'I——' Thrown by the change of conversation, Faith reached into the pocket of her trousers for her notebook. 'There are a couple——' she started to say, but the little lady in front of her held up a 'stop' hand.

'There's nothing more important to a girl than getting married,' she pontificated. 'Dicky told me that—and

Dicky was always right. You should wear dresses, you know. Trousers are neat, but—— Something alluring.'

Oh, brother, Faith told herself grimly. Marriage and children. She winced, and decided to attack. 'And then there's *domina*, milady. I would prefer to be called Miss Faith.'

'I'm sure you would.' Another giggle. 'We make few changes here, *domina*. But if you want the lower servants to call you Miss Faith—— Such lovely hair you have. Dicky would have loved you. Dear Dicky, how I miss him. "Don't ever change a thing, Sunny," he told me on his death-bed. And I never have!'

'Yes, well——' Faith took a deep breath and referred to her notebook. 'There are several problems——' she started to say.

'I'm sure there are.' Lady Sunny held up that 'stop' hand again. 'Which you will solve most satisfactorily. Each of us has our place in life, my dear. Yours is problem-solving. Do you like fair-haired men?'

'Time for your pills, milady,' the maid said. Lady Sunny slid off her pouffe and was gone before Faith Latimore had a chance to say or ask another word.

'Close your mouth; you'll be catching flies any minute,' Faith told herself. The man who appeared to gather up the kittens looked at her curiously. 'There has to be some method for unraveling a situation like this,' she insisted. The man nodded.

Faith wandered down the veranda toward what might well be called the bow of the villa. Straight ahead of her was the deep dip down into the flat plain where Basseterre town sparkled. Across the bay loomed the peak of Nevis. And another maid came running.

'Miss Faith,' the girl called. The word gets around fast, Faith told herself as she rearranged her face. 'By the boat. There is a man!'

'Oh?'

The maid twisted away like a miniature whirlwind and was gone as well.

'I don't know when I've seen quicker servants,' Faith muttered as she lengthened her stride and found the ramp leading down to the sea. There were no stairs; everything was ramps. All of the servants spoke with a touch of Irish brogue. Rose Cottage had fifty-six rooms. Nothing seemed to make sense. But the girl was right. There *was* a man! A rather tall man, for a fact, well-muscled. Since he was wearing nothing but a pair of ragged gray shorts *that* was easy to determine. 'MEN'. That was the title of the first page in her guidance book, the one that had waited for her on the plane. Evidently Lady Sunny had some problem with 'MEN'. Me, too, Faith thought, and steeled herself.

Bleached blond hair—cut short; smooth-shaven; sparkling white teeth, being displayed now in a deep grin. He offered her a sweeping bow. 'You can't be Lady Sunny?'

'You're so right,' Faith responded. 'I can't be. But who can *you* be?'

'Well, I'll be—— A Yankee!' He came out of the shadows and stood with feet spread apart, hands on hips. Green eyes, she catalogued. Glittering like some sort of rogue.

'You wanted something to do with our boat?'

It was the first time Faith had been down in the dock area, and her mind was on him, not the boat. He gestured vaguely behind him. 'Ship,' he said, 'not a boat. The damn thing is a World War II patrol craft. I didn't realize that the lady had her own navy.'

Faith Latimore almost swallowed her tongue and looked. All true. The ship towered over her like a gray ghost, and stretched down the pier-side until the shadows from the cliff blotted it out. 'And just how,' she asked firmly, 'does that concern you?'

'I think I'll take that up with Lady Sunny,' he said, just as firmly.

Those green eyes sparked at her. What was he thinking? I have an important problem, and I'm not going to take this up with some servant? Well, two could play at that game!

'And that,' Faith returned, like a hard-driven backhand tennis stroke, 'will be a cold day in autumn. Milady doesn't see casual strangers. If you would care to write, giving your reasons, someone will evaluate your request, Mr——?'

'Holson,' he offered. 'Harry Holson. And who is it that will evaluate my request, Miss——?'

'Latimore,' she said, ignoring his extended hand. 'Faith Latimore.'

'Latimore,' he mused. 'A famous name in the construction business.'

'It's a popular name. We are a very large family Stateside, Mr Holson.'

'You don't have to call in your troops,' he snapped. He edged toward the path that led around the house and down on to the plain. Faith looked around. Behind her, silent but watching, was one of the husky male servants that staffed the waterfront.

'O'Malley,' the large one introduced himself.

Faith turned around again to follow the progress of Mr Holson as he swaggered down the paved path that led to the only road along the south shore of St Kitts.

'He's the boss-man at the new hotel construction, *domina*. Very important in town. Strange, that. There's an older man of the same name what comes on occasion to call on Lady Sunny. Related, you suppose?'

Faith shook her head and shrugged her shoulders. One more puzzle to solve? The world was filled with strangers, and she already had more puzzles than solutions. Maybe it hadn't been the smartest thing to do, dismissing him so quickly.

'Is he going to walk all the way back to Basseterre?' She took a deep breath. 'Mr Holson!' she yelled.

He stopped and turned. She waved at him. He sauntered back up the path. 'Yes? You called?'

'Surely you don't intend to walk all the way back to the capital city?'

'It's not as many kilometers as all that. Besides, what are the alternatives?'

'You could——' She took a deep breath. It was not, after all, her home. 'You could stay for lunch, and we could have our chauffeur drive you back.'

'That's the best offer I've had all week.' The smile was back on his face, a sort of lopsided smile that had all the aspects of a con man's grin. But Faith couldn't care less. The cottage was a lonely place for someone from the outside, and perhaps he could answer a couple of her thousand and one questions if treated nicely. She took his arm and tugged him toward the ramp. Her bodyguard tagged along behind.

'But is it true that ours is a ship of war?' She cocked her head to look up at him.

'It's a warship all right. Still carrying some armament,' Holson said. 'Why don't you ask your guard?'

Faith looked back over her shoulder for an answer. Harry Holson guided her to a stop to keep her from running off the path.

'I the auto man—and the seaman. They call me O'Malley.'

Faith shifted her attention. 'A warship, Mr O'Malley?'

He grinned, displaying a mouth full of huge teeth.

'After the Great War, *domina*,' he said with a bow from the waist. 'Mr Dicky, he always wanted to be admiral, you know, but failed the eye-tests. So he bought this excess Navy ship and hired a crew.' A pause, as if debating a secret he *had* to divulge.

'But both he and Lady Sunny, they gets seasick on t'first cruise, you understand. So they build this dock, tie up the boat, and use it for parties and such. And then the captain, he gets homesick and leaves, and the mate, he marries, and gradually everyone else but me goes away. So I am the seaman.'

'But you know how to sail the ship?'

'Me, *domina*? I am the wiper. I wipes the engines every day, and polishes the rails. Mr Dicky, he ups and dies years ago, and he says to Lady Sunny, "Don't change a thing." So I still wipes the engine and polishes the rails. Every day except Saturday and Sunday.'

Faith Latimore felt a headache coming on. 'Yes,' she said, not understanding a single thing. 'I understand— I think.'

Holson's arm tugged at her. She squeezed his hand tight, for fear she might fall off the world. But it was only the first step upward, and he had such an infectious grin!

'No elevator?' he asked about halfway up.

'No,' she sighed. 'Lady Sunny doesn't go anywhere. Her late husband told her——'

'I know—"don't ever change a thing"!'

'You don't have to be sarcastic about it!' She tugged him to a stop and glared up at him. 'I would appreciate it if you would not laugh at Lady Sunny or her way of life.'

'You look threatening when you frown.' He tilted her chin up again with his forefinger. A massive forefinger. 'She *never* goes out?'

'That's just one of a thousand questions I can't answer,' she said, sighing. 'I feel so—inadequate— around here.'

'Ask me one of them. I might know the answer.'

And why not? she thought. He's a stranger. I can't possibly expose all my stupidities in one question! 'So tell me, why do all the servants speak with an Irish brogue?'

'That's an easy one.' They had reached the level of the veranda. One of the maids was standing at the entrance. 'Brunch, please,' he said, and then turned back to Faith.

'All your servants were hired from the island of Montserrat. Cromwell ordered Northern Ireland settled by Scottish Presbyterians back in the 1600s. The most rebellious of the native Irish, he shipped off to places like Montserrat. The brogue is still heard, especially among the peasants. And the Irish harp is inscribed on the island's flag!'

Faith fumbled for words, and found nothing available. 'My!' she finally summarized. 'My goodness!'

There was a small clatter behind her. She whirled around. O'Malley, not having been dismissed, was assisting the maid in setting up a small round table next to the rail.

'You seem to be very closely acquainted with the cottage servants,' she commented. 'You've been here before?'

'A time or two,' he admitted as he pulled out her chair. 'When we first started our development project in Frigate Bay, the head of our organization took me around to meet all the social wheels. It helps when the local manager is on speaking terms with the important people.'

'Do you say so?' Faith murmured. 'That would be with Mr—Holson?'

'That's the one.'

'A big, tall broth of a man?'

He gave her a curious look. 'You know my father?'

'In a distant sort of way,' she admitted. 'We Latimores are a huge worldwide clan. But then you knew Lady Sunny, and yet you——'

'No,' he said, sighing. 'We came back twice, but Lady Sunny was down with a bad cold, so instead we met Miss Pearl, the—what did they call her?'

'*Domina*. The one in charge. And what happened to Miss Pearl?'

'Why, she got married. They all do. I think there have been three or four *dominas* in the past several years or so. Lady Sunny believes in matrimony. Didn't you know?'

Faith could feel the alarm bells go off in her ears. Matrimony? Why did I leave home? To get away from my sisters and their urgent call to arms? Or my mother, who was no agitator at all, but did occasionally drop a word or two about marriage? And who was it that provided my introduction to that London solicitor? My father, that's who! Big, lovable Bruce Latimore! Dear old Dad!

'Damn,' she muttered.

The maid at her elbow drew back. '*Domina* does not care for toast and eggs this morning?'

I've got to get my ears checked, Faith told herself. With the off-shore wind blowing, she found it almost impossible to hear any of the servants as they bustled around. 'Yes, *domina* cares very much for eggs and toast. And what are you having, Mr Holson?'

'Steak and eggs,' he announced. 'And call me Harry. All my friends do.'

'How nice for you, Mr Holson.'

He waited for just about the blink of an eye and, when nothing further was forthcoming, shrugged his shoulders and picked up his fork.

Faith watched him from the corner of her eye. 'You can tell more about a man by watching him eat,' her

mother insisted, 'than you can by talking to him for
hours.' And maybe there was something to it. Her mother
was one very smart woman! Dear Mary Kate!

'You've been on St Kitts for some time, Mr Holson?'

He sighed and put down his knife. Mistake number
ten, Faith thought. Here's a man who wants to concentrate on eating, and then talk later. If talking was what
he ever had in mind, that was.

'About a year,' he mumbled as he desperately tried to
chew the steak and talk at the same time. A massive
swallow cleared his throat.

'And before that?'

'Texas.' He looked at her as if hoping she might
swallow her tongue. Faith almost obliged. He really was
a nice-looking man. Smooth skin, closely shaved, hair
neatly trimmed. Biceps enlarged enough to indicate he
didn't spend *all* his time with a slide-rule. He intercepted
her examination.

'I don't normally come to call dressed like this. It just
happens that this is my regular day off——'

'And you're slumming?'

'More like slimming.' He grinned at her, a repetition
of that big, infectious look. 'Besides, everyone on the
island knows that Lady Sunny's house is the most scenic
attraction on the island.' A pause, as he swept his plate
clean and followed with a sip of coffee.

'Texas?' She mulled it over in her mind. 'I have a
sister who lives in Texas. On the Bryan Quinn ranch up
in the Panhandle. Do you know it?'

Another one of those startled looks. 'Know it? It's
the biggest ranch in the Panhandle. When I was working
my way through college I had a part-time job with them
during round-up.'

'Now that's interesting. You must have known everything there was to know about horses?'

He looked blank.

'Texas? Round-up? Horses?'

'Oh, that. You're a little behind the times, little lady. How about Texas, round-up, helicopters?' The grin again, and then a sniffing of the air. 'What the hell is that I smell?'

Faith took a sniff or two to check. 'Oh, that. Lady Sunny is susceptible to colds and fevers—and mosquitoes. So twice a day we spray the cottage with a rose-scented bug spray. So you fly helicopters?'

'Any brand, any size, any color,' he retorted, and then sneezed a massive sneeze. 'But I'm allergic to a lot of things, and I suspect your bug spray is one of them.' He reached into his back pocket and pulled out a massive red and white bandana. 'I've got to go!' He scraped back his chair, only to find O'Malley already behind him, moving the light bamboo chair out of his way. Faith moved her chair back by herself, gently, and stood up.

'That's another one of our house rules,' she told him. 'No chair-scraping. Lady Sunny's husband believed that a bamboo chair should be able to last for fifty years if it wasn't scraped or rattled or bruised.'

His eyes were watering, and the bandana was ineffective. 'There's a rule for everything?' he inquired hoarsely.

'Not quite. And besides, they're not rules, they're customs. The spraying was concocted by Lady Sunny's husband to protect her from diseases, and——'

'I know,' he said, sighing. 'And she never changes a thing.' Faith beamed at him. 'Where is the old—lady now?'

'Well, as it happens, milady is allergic to the spray—as you are—so she always retires to her shoe-room before the spraying begins.' Faith consulted her wristwatch. 'And you have reason to be disturbed. They're spraying five minutes early!'

'I see.' He backed out toward the railing, where an eddy of a breeze offered some help. 'Her husband had his chemists concoct a spray to protect her from bugs, only she's allergic—to the spray, not the bugs—but she'll never change it because her husband is——'

'Was.'

'Yes. He *was* always right, so she retires to her shoe-room?'

'Just so. You catch on so very quickly, Mr Holson.'

'Shoe-room?'

'Well, she has to have some place to store the shoes. Her factories are very busy. They send her two pairs of every new shoe design they originate. Since that amounts to about a thousand new designs a year, worldwide, she has a considerable stock in her little "museum". And she feels she just can't throw them away. Once every two years her factory managers come one at a time to visit, and of course their particular shoes——'

He held up a hand, reminiscent of Lady Sunny herself. 'Yes, I understand. Lord, what an attic you all must have.'

'Not quite. She refers to the room as her "library" or her "museum",' she corrected mildly. 'O'Malley. We must get Mr Holson back to his work. Would you bring the car around?'

'The—car?' The chauffeur hesitated for a moment, and then displayed his massive white teeth. 'Yes, the car.' And he loped off down the length of the porch and down the ramp.

'I think if we go along down to the garage, Mr Holson, we might walk our way out of the spray, and——'

'Harry,' he suggested again. 'My name is Harry. I'd appreciate it if you'd call me Harry.'

'Harry, I'll call you Harry.' Faith gave in.

'Please, let's get moving toward the garage before I choke on the spray.' They walked down the path from the patio and turned before the cliff-edge. 'Why did you give in so easily?' Harry asked.

'Give in?' Faith questioned.

'Yes,' Harry remarked. 'Give in. As in concluding that you could safely use my first name. Or do you believe that we won't be seeing each other again?'

'I don't see why I should see you again,' Faith said, just a little upset that he could read her so easily.

'We will be seeing each other again,' Harry said with conviction.

'Why?'

'Because St Kitts is a very small island. And Lady Sunny is a dedicated matchmaker.'

'Why,' Faith asked, 'do you feel that Lady Sunny will be bringing us together in the future?'

'Just call it instinct.'

By this time they had come to the garage. There was no car running in front of it and the doors were closed and locked. O'Malley came around the edge of the building. He came and stood by them in front of the garage doors.

'Where's the car, O'Malley?' Faith wondered. 'We do have a car, don't we?'

'Yes, ma'am,' O'Malley said cheerfully. 'We got a car. Fine car.'

'Where is it?' Faith asked quietly.

'It's in the garage, ma'am.'

'Mr O'Malley, are you, in fact, the chauffeur?' Faith wanted to be very sure she was going to scream at the right person.

'Yes, ma'am, I'm chauffeur. And we got a very fine car.' O'Malley paused at this point and looked Faith in the eyes. 'But our fine car is not on the road for almost twenty year.'

'Where is this vintage automobile?' Faith spoke slowly, trying to be very precise. O'Malley's ready answer had robbed her of anger and substituted curiosity.

'It's here in garage,' O'Malley said as he took a big key out of his pocket and unlocked the door. The door was almost stuck closed and Harry helped O'Malley apply a little weight. The door hinges screeched in protest and a number of birds flew out the opening. Obviously there was a hole in the roof somewhere.

'I guess that these doors haven't been opened since the car was put inside,' Harry commented with a smile. And then the lights came on in the garage. Sitting on blocks was a beautiful pink 1950 Cadillac. With whitewall tires. All one could see was the rear end. But it didn't matter to Harry. He was in love with the car at first sight. It was a classic, and he was a car-bug.

While Harry was admiring the vehicle, Faith stared at O'Malley. 'Okay, O'Malley.' She went back to the original question. 'Why haven't you driven the car in all these years?'

'Last time it went out, Master Dicky took it for a spin,' O'Malley said with a grin. 'Master Dicky wasn't a good driver. He ran into a cow and dented the front end very badly. Of the car, that is.'

'Obviously,' Harry commented from the front end of the car, 'Master Dicky was going at some speed.' He looked up at O'Malley and they exchanged grins. 'He managed to crack the engine block.'

'Why didn't anyone fix the car?' Faith asked, although she already knew the answer. 'Is this another one of those "don't change anything" items?'

'Yes, ma'am. It happen in the Trouble. Nobody has time to fix it then. Besides, Master Dicky has had enough of the car. More than enough.'

'Well, Mr Holson,' Faith said with regret in her voice, 'I seem to have offered a ride before I knew the cir-

cumstances.' She turned to O'Malley. 'Is there some sort
of transportation available to Mr Holson to take him
back to Basseterre?'

'Yes, ma'am,' O'Malley was quick to assure her.
'We've got a fine pony cart. I can hitch it up in no time.'

'Why don't you do that, then?'

O'Malley went quickly out the doors toward another
building, leaving Harry and Faith among the cobwebs
and dust of years. Suddenly, Faith felt a little uncertain.
She looked around her, mainly to keep from looking at
the figure of Harry Holson. 'My mother would have a
fit if she came into this place,' she said.

'Why?' Harry startled her. She didn't know he'd
moved from the car to her side.

'My mother,' Faith said with a fond smile, 'has the
firm belief that everything should have a place and those
places should be filled. Dust and cobwebs are not allowed in houses. She would declare war on any signs of
neglect.'

'I know what you mean,' Harry said, looking around.
'My granny had the same fight going.'

He was too close, Faith thought. Too close and too
big and too—naked. Luckily for her peace of mind she
heard the harness jingle outside the open doors. 'Your
ride is here.' She walked out of the garage into the sun-
light and stood facing the equipage. It was an Irish
jaunting-car, with seats on both sides of the axle so that
passengers rode back to back with the driver facing
forward.

'Are you coming with us?' Harry asked over her
shoulder. 'It looks like O'Malley hitched up one large
cart.'

'I'd have to ask Lady Sunny for permission to leave
the estate,' Faith murmured, 'and I don't have any
reason to go.'

'Sure you do,' Harry said confidently. 'How long have you been on the island?'

'Five days.'

'Have you left the estate in all that time?' Harry was trying to get at something, she could tell. Unfortunately, he was bending closer as he spoke and that almost shorted out her brain connection.

'I—I had a taxi ride from the airport,' Faith stammered.

'Please,' Harry said, sounding affronted. 'You have seen nothing of this tropical island paradise. You have to get off the estate. Why don't you track Lady Sunny down and get permission? O'Malley and I'll wait here, telling each other lies.' He smiled at the large driver, who smiled right back.

Faith needed little urging. 'I won't be long,' she shouted as she sprinted toward the house ramp. Suddenly, she was in a hurry to see St Kitts. To say nothing about traveling with Harry Holson. Maybe she could see where he lived. Maybe she could see him with a shirt on. She pounded up the ramp, startling the maids and the butler, and climbed the massive curved marble walkway that led up to the center of the house. Then it was down again to where the library stood.

Faith fumbled her way to the door of the air-conditioned, climate-controlled vault in which Lady Sunny kept her shoes. Lady Sunny's maid answered the door and reluctantly let Faith inside. It was Faith's first visit.

The white walls were lined with brown steel shoe cabinets. One of them was open. Faith could see that there were four panels inside the cabinet so that there were four shoe-racks per side. Lady Sunny could keep massive numbers of shoes in this room. And it was built for comfort. There was a round couch in the middle of the room, covered in soft satin. The floor was carpeted wall-to-wall in a deep, beige rug. When one walked on the rug, one reached uneasily for something to hold on to for balance.

Lady Sunny was in front of the cabinet she'd opened and was inspecting several pairs of shoes. It was then that Faith noticed a small peculiarity. The shoes were all of different design and construction, but were all light blue, with inset diamanté in the toes and heels.

Milady looked up and smiled at Faith. 'You haven't been running, have you, *domina*? It's not ladylike. It raises perspiration. Ladies don't perspire.'

'Milady,' Faith said quietly as she bobbed a curtsy, 'please excuse my appearance, but I ran to see if you'd permit me to accompany O'Malley while we drive a guest back to Basseterre.'

'What guest?' Lady Sunny's attention had drifted back to her shoes. 'I didn't know we had any guests.'

'Yes, ma'am, I know that,' Faith reassured her. 'This young man was down looking at the boat——'

'Ship, my dear,' Lady Sunny interrupted gently. 'I'm sure it's called a ship. Dicky was so proud of our ship.' A reflective pause as she turned one of the shoes over in her hands. 'I think of Dicky so often when I'm among my shoes. He designed the first pair, you know.'

'Ship,' Faith repeated, her mouth hanging half-open.

'What young man is that, my dear?'

'The tall, blond man who wasn't wearing a shirt.'

'Oh, yes, Mr Holson.' Lady Sunny's attention shifted back to Faith, and she eyed the young woman with a gleam in her eye. 'I remember that young man well. How unfortunate that he would come calling just when I'm too busy to see him. Of course, my dear, please drive with him. O'Malley will be a suitable chaperon.'

'I could inventory the shoes for you,' Faith offered rather tentatively, 'and then you could visit with——'

'Nonsense,' the lady said. 'Go on, my dear; don't keep the young man waiting.' With that, she took Faith's arm and escorted her to the door at flank speed. 'A hat,' Lady Sunny commented. 'Be sure to wear a hat with a wide brim. The sun is dangerous, my dear.'

Faith found herself on the outside of the room with the door closed before she could take a deep breath. And what, she asked herself, is *that* all about? Is young Harry romancing the obviously rich lady? Or is it his father, as yet unseen, who would like to get his hands on her shoe empire?

Or is this all a set-up to get *me* married, with dear old Dad the sponsor, and Lady Sunny his clandestine companion? It's not my mother, thank God. *She* would *never* conspire to marry me off. Or would she? Oh, lord. Go carefully, Faith.

And with that she cast off all the plots from her mind—all but one. It was her duty, according to her contract, to protect Lady Sunny from gigolos. Was that really a word these days? According to her guide-book it was Faith's *major* duty. And as of the moment only Harry Holson presented himself as the classic villain.

It was a thoughtful young Latimore who walked down to the pony cart where Harry was waiting.

CHAPTER TWO

THE green, two-wheeled pony cart was waiting in the shade of the garage when Faith came panting down the ramp, trailing her hat. 'Have I kept you waiting?' The hat was beyond her. Not for years had she worn a hat. Not since her mother, Mary Kate, used to gather up all the girls of a Sunday and march them off to church. Back in East Attleboro that had been, back in Massachusetts. Back before she'd won her argument against being an engineer and turned to law for a living.

Harry got up in leisurely fashion from the grass and smiled at her. His battered denims had acquired a massive grass stain. He brushed at the spot ineffectively, and then gave up. 'Not at all. I'm ready,' he said, 'O'Malley's ready, but I'm not sure about Isabelle.'

'Isabelle?'

'The horse, Miss Faith.' O'Malley, who had been standing at the horse's head, feeding it handfuls of long grass, came around to the side to help her mount up. He had caught the word about her name in her absence. Harry Holson, intent on the same errand, came from the opposite direction. They were both big men; both grabbed for Faith Latimore and the resultant collision shook the old cart. Isabelle whinnied and moved a step or two down the path, pulling the cart away from where Faith, suspended in the air between the two big men, hung precipitously.

She took a deep breath and squeaked, 'Help,' but very softly. After all, she already had more help available than

25

she could ever use. O'Malley grinned and withdrew from the competition.

Harry, with both hands spanning her waist, hesitated for a moment, as if he had some other goal in mind. 'I don't suppose you mean to carry me all the way to Basseterre?' she prompted. He came out of his daze.

'Carry? Oh, no, not at all. You're a very——'

'I wish you wouldn't say anything more,' she told him primly. 'I'm a big woman, and I fully realize what all that means. And if you would put me down now I wouldn't be showing all my—all my unmentionables to the neighborhood. Please?'

He grinned as he set her down on the bench seat. The cart tilted slightly on its automobile tires. She ducked her head to fit under the canopy which provided some scant shade. He started to hoist himself up on to the cart beside her. O'Malley yelled a warning and the cart almost tipped over.

'Balance,' the chauffeur called as Harry vaulted off the wagon. 'One on each side.'

'You mean I have to ride all the way to Basseterre back to back with this lovely lady?'

'That's the way,' O'Malley agreed. 'It ain't but only five miles. Everybody ready?'

He snapped the reins. Isabelle, with her head down in the lush grass, turned and looked over her shoulder. Glared over her shoulder, to be truthful. Faith squirmed around to look at the animal. Isabelle was a small piebald of hardly fourteen hands, with a swayback that spelled old age in capital letters.

'Gidap!' O'Malley yelled, and reached for his buggy whip. The horse, obviously not threatened by it at all, leaned into the traces and the cart began to roll. Down off the side of the hill they went, across the railroad tracks, through the streets of Challengers Town, down to the flat plain that girdled the Caribbean Sea, down to where the eternal sea-breezes blew and cooled. Faith took off her wide-brimmed hat and let the fingers of the wind blow through her hair.

'Hey,' Harry Holson called. 'Keep your hat on. Sunstroke is endemic in the tropics. And did you remember your sunscreen?'

'I don't see you doing all that,' she shouted back at him. 'I suppose sunstroke is strictly a female disease?'

'No, but I've been here for more than a year,' he returned. The cart rocked as Holson stood up on his side and reseated himself sidewise on the bench. All of which put him within reaching distance of Faith. She considered for just a second. She could jump off the cart, which was not an attractive solution, or she could stay where she was and let his arm fall around her shoulders—which was not exactly a bad idea, come to think of it. She turned sidewise, tucking her legs up, and challenged him to do his worst. Or best?

'So, what about the guided tour?' she asked.

'Who, me? I'm a stranger here myself.' He sprawled out on the bench seat, feet up, mimicking her. A nice arrangement, Faith told herself. Now they were both riding side by side, looking forward. His arm came just around her shoulders. It was—comfortable.

'Now we in Trinity Parish,' O'Malley announced. 'And it be Sunday, Mr Holson, and you——'

'I know, I know,' he grumbled. 'Sunday in Trinity Parish.' He shrugged himself around and pulled a thin T-shirt from his pocket. 'Blue laws,' he grumbled in Faith's direction as he stuffed himself into the shirt. 'Whole island is divided into thirteen parishes——'

'Fourteen,' O'Malley interrupted.

'Yeah, fourteen. They make the local laws, the way the counties do back home.'

'But—there's hardly room for them to be counties.'

'The island is five miles wide—in a few places—and twenty-three miles long,' he said. 'But they *do* make the local laws. And the closer you get to Basseterre, the more strict the dress codes become. Especially on Sunday. And that's our radio and television station.' He gestured toward the north where a tall, thin tower crowned the flat-topped peak that crowded the road. 'We have a contract to add a second television channel next year.'

'Busy, busy, busy,' she chortled. But you came on this ride to get information, she reprimanded herself. Information! Get it all down. Is his father the wolf working against Lady Sunny's Red Riding Hood? Get to work! 'Does your father live here with you?'

'Well, not hardly.' How did his arm get around my shoulder? she asked herself. She shifted uneasily, and the cart rocked.

'Miss Faith,' O'Malley cautioned. 'You gotta sit still in pony cart. Isabelle is one very old horse. She don't take to rolling back an' forth.'

Faith accepted the admonishment and tried to steer the conversation back on to her own grounds. 'But I thought you and your father——'

'Oh, he comes around,' Holson said. 'We're a pretty big company, you know. He has a base of operations in San Juan, in Puerto Rico.'

'Comes to inspect your work, I suspect?'

Holson laughed. 'Comes to inspect *something*,' he said. 'But not necessarily my work.' Faith turned her head to catch his facial expression, but the sun was in her eyes.

'And what does your mother think about that?'

He shook his head dolefully, and this time she caught the gleam in his eyes. 'My mother died on my tenth birthday,' he said solemnly. 'Twenty-five years ago.'

'Oh——' Flustered, she hardly knew what to say. 'I'm sorry to hear that. I wouldn't want to pry——'

'The hell you wouldn't,' he said, chuckling. That arm was back again, snaking around her shoulders, and leaving one hand to rest just below her shoulder, just above her breast. It gave an awesome touch. She stiffened. Silence.

The clip-clop of Isabelle's hooves played counterpoint with the wild screams of the fishing gulls just offshore. The road ran flat as a die, in some places a mere hundred yards from the Caribbean. The tops of a cluster of palmetto palms nodded in the breeze between them and the shore. Brilliant green brush climbed the sides of the mountain to their north.

And still Faith persisted. 'Does your father come over to St Kitts very often?'

'About once a week,' he said, and then chuckled again.

'What's funny about that?' she snapped.

'*Domina*, I do believe you're fishing for information about my father. He'd be delighted to know.'

Faith shifted to the far edge of the seat and turned up her nose at him. Her pearl cheeks were red, and not from the sun. His arm trailed her and caught up. She turned to stare at him. 'I don't mind telling you anything you want to know,' he said solemnly. 'You don't have to fence around. Straight questions. How old am I? Thirty-five years old. How old is my father? Sixty-three years old. I might add he's a very virile sixty-three. I expect to call him tomorrow. Should I mention your interest?'

'Don't you dare,' she snapped at him as she turned to stare at the mountain for want of anything else to stare at. He could see her shoulders shaking.

'Oh, well,' he murmured. 'I've been wrong before.'

'I'll bet you have,' she muttered at him. 'Lots of times!'

'An' this we passing be West Farm Estate,' O'Malley announced mournfully. 'They make plenty sugar here in the old days. No more.'

'Nobody makes plenty sugar any more,' Harry Holson interjected. 'They all make *some* sugar. My father has plans to add a dozen tourist areas to spark the trade. Cotton used to be a mainstay, but that's almost done now. Too much worldwide competition. We've a fairly large development going in Frigate Bay. We've already put up some first-class family homes, and now we're working on a hotel.'

Faith did her best to shut off all communications with the pair of them. O'Malley had become a co-conspirator. She could feel it in her bones. But then, she reminded herself, all her experience with men indicted them as blatant co-conspirators! She shrugged her shoulders and pulled inside herself—and thereby missed the next excitement.

Isabelle, for all her age and antiquity, took a couple of stutter-steps and began to move off at a trot.

'What the hell...?' Harry Holson ejaculated.

'Train,' O'Malley said. 'Nine o'clock train. You can feel it coming.'

Harry consulted his watch. 'Eleven forty-five,' he reported.

'Like I said,' O'Malley repeated, 'nine o'clock train. Right on time.' He braced his feet and tightened his hold on the reins. 'Fool horse! Cut that out. You ain't no pony no more!'

'Something more than a train coming,' Harry said.

'That fool boy at Friendly's,' O'Malley reported. 'Racin' car. We got maybe four thousand cars and trucks on these islands, and that boy have a Maserati. I think we better——' The chauffeur was using all his strength trying to pull the horse in, with little luck.

Isabelle moved from a trot to a troublesome run, continuously looking back over her left shoulder. Faith swiveled around on the bench seat, facing backward. A cloud of dust blotted out the road some half a mile

behind them. At the core of the cloud was a little red
button of a car, with motor accelerating into a high-
pitched buzz. From the railroad track which paralleled
the road, the nose of a 2-4-2 narrow gauge black locomotive rocketed along out of the car's dust. The tracks
on which it raced bounced up and down. Black smoke
blasted from its stack.

'Crazy,' O'Malley shouted. 'They racing for the
crossing! Isabelle is going to——'

The shrill whistle of the locomotive matched the deeper
roar of the car's horn, and Isabelle was no longer "going
to". She gathered herself up, swerved off the road at
high speed, and crashed down into the little gulch that
separated the road from the railroad on the left-hand
side. O'Malley, yelling like a charioteer, stood up and
leaned back on the reins. The car and the train went by
them on either side. Isabelle sawed herself to a stop.
O'Malley went over the front of the cart and skidded
into the deep grass. Faith took a deep breath and buried
her head in her arms as she took flight off to one side.
And graciously fainted.

Faith Latimore gradually opened one eye—cautiously.
A female head translated into 'sister'.

'Ah, you are with us?' A soft contralto voice. Hands
fussed with her sheet, smoothing it gently over her
shoulders. And, with more data available, *that* translated into 'hospital'.

'Just—where?'

'The JN France General Hospital, on the outskirts of
Basseterre. I'm Sister Robinson. How are you feeling?'

'Thirsty.'

'Of course. Ice water?'

A plastic straw swiveled around, trying to find her
mouth. Her lips clamped down on its end and she inhaled. 'Ah. Good.'

The pair of them beamed at each other, and suddenly Faith's eye struggled and closed. Not for sleep; just for thought.

'O'Malley?' she asked, from out of the darkness.

'Scratches, nothing more.' The sister was puttering around the room, rearranging this or that.

'And——' She hesitated at the name.

'Mr Holson?'

'Yes.' Followed by a sigh. 'Harry?'

'Mr Holson is a man with infinite experience with bumps and bruises. He required four Band-Aids, and then went off, raging.'

'Raging?'

The sister offered her another sip from the straw. 'Yes, raging. Mr Holson is a man of great emotions. The young man in the car, he didn't even stop to see if you were well. I suspect he will regret that before nightfall.'

'My goodness!' Faith managed to squeeze open one eye again. The room was somewhat darker. The venetian blinds had been partially drawn, casting soothing shadows. 'I've never had a White Knight before. Do you suppose he will do the boy some hurt?'

'Undoubtedly.'

'I seem to have somewhat of a headache,' she said in a very small voice.

Another voice intervened, a low, gruff male voice. 'So you are the wonder woman that's turning our island upside-down?'

Faith tried both eyes and barely managed to make it. The sister was big—taller than she had expected. The man was short and slightly rotund, with a massive smile on his face and not a hair on top of his head.

'Dr Ottley, my dear. You have a headache—and a small concussion. Plus a round dozen scratches, and some black and blue spots which will look marvelously green in a day or so. Nothing serious. You can probably go home tomorrow. Lady Sunny has called four times already. My lady stands by her associates, you know. In two hours she has called the Prime Minister, the chief of police, the chairman of the railroad board, the president of the hospital, and the Governor-General.'

The doctor took a deep breath and wiped his forehead with a massive white handkerchief. 'If Queen Elizabeth didn't live so far away I'm sure she'd also be on the calling list. The good lady assures me that she and the Queen Mother are related. Fifth cousins, did she say?' He shook his head dolefully. 'Sometimes it is difficult to treat famous patients. A doctor's life is not altogether pleasantries and Wednesday golf.' He looked altogether mournful, but out of the corner of her good eye Faith could see that the nurse was hiding a grin.

'Well, then, my dear. Rest well, eat a good supper——'

'And Isabelle?' Faith interrupted.

'Oh, dear.' The doctor fussed anxiously. 'Is there another patient? I've overlooked someone?'

'The horse,' the nurse coached from the sidelines.

'The horse?' He scratched the back of his head. 'I don't do horses.'

'An injured leg,' the sister supplied. 'She's already back at the villa. You're running late, doctor.'

'To be sure,' the doctor muttered. 'Be calm. Nothing stressful.' He snatched up his bag and fled. Both the women watched as the door slammed shut behind him.

The sister shrugged her shoulders. 'More water?'

'Is everyone on this island crazy?'

'No, only about a third,' the sister replied. 'Too much sun. Easy now. If you keep moving your head you'll feel dizzy. There's a good girl.'

Faith, who had not felt like a 'good girl' in many a year, sighed again. 'I think I could use some sleep,' she murmured.

'The call button is——'

The door burst open, and a delightfully bandaged O'Malley came in, interrupting the sister. 'Oh—Sister. Pardon, but I must speak with *domina*.' He came over to the bed.

'The horse, she will not pull a trap again, *domina*. I send her out to pasture. The wagon is a total ruin. Milady—I hear her saying that if you are not out soon of the hospital, she will leave the villa and confront the Governor and tell him something—something nasty. But there is no conveyance to take her to the city. Shall I buy a new wagon? We could rent a horse without any——'

'No. Nothing like that.'

'But—if milady desires to go and there is no conveyance? Never have we had such a difficulty. Not since Mr Dicky has died! What a shame!'

'Please, O'Malley. My head hurts. Quietly, now. Can you drive a car?'

'An automobile? Certain sure. Domina Martha is ten years ago. She says to me, "Change nothing, Mr Dicky says. But be *ready* to change," Domina Martha says! Once a week for the past ten years I take the driving instructions downtown. Murphy and Kravitz, the garage, that is. I have the license and all. But no auto.'

'In my wallet,' Faith said. 'Credit cards. Go and buy us a very large limousine. Light blue. We'll have the diamanté added on later. Bring it here to the hospital. Can you do that?'

'I can do that, *domina*. But there is no need of credit cards. All I need to say is—for Lady Sunny. One limousine is enough?'

'Oh, lord,' Faith Latimore sighed. Not even the Latimore millions would be enough. 'For the moment!'

O'Malley offered up a tremendous grin. 'You bring interesting times, *domina*,' he said as he disappeared out the door.

'Well, now,' Sister Robinson commented softly. 'Now it is sleep-time. The entire island will be in an uproar when the story gets around!'

'That's what I'm afraid of,' Faith murmured. 'My instructions from London were, "Don't raise a fuss!"'

It was five o'clock when Faith woke again, not knowing whether it was the noise in the hall or the striking of the clock in the tower in Independence Square that brought her head round. Sister Robinson zoomed into the room and shut the door carefully behind her. She leaned against the closed door, breathing hard.

'*Domina*? You are awake?'

'What else?' Faith commented. 'That clock sounds—— Yes, I'm awake. What's the confusion?'

'Your Mr Holson is back, along with a young man and a policeman. You would wish to see them?'

Now that's a question to debate, Faith told herself. Harry Holson? I don't know exactly why, but it would be a pleasure to see him again. And a policeman? Why not? 'Why not?' she said. The sister paused, as if she was afraid to open the door. When she did so she stepped to one side to avoid the crowd. It was really only three people, but it seemed much bigger. Harry led the procession straight to her bedside.

'This is Vincent Declaur,' Harry announced. Faith shifted her eyes. Declaur was a big, pimply young man, who was dragged in front of her by his shirt collar. He was bigger than Harry Holson by some three or four inches and twenty pounds. It could not be said that he came willingly.

'Is this the man——?' the policeman started to ask, only to be overridden by Harry Holson.

'This is the kid in the Maserati,' Harry said.

Faith managed to raise herself up on her elbows. Sister Robinson came swiftly around to the bed to help. The young man looked somewhat battered.

'With all that speed you lost the race to the train?' It was hard not to be sympathetic. He looked to be a wreck.

'Oh, I beat the train all right,' Declaur said dolefully. 'But Mr Holson—him I couldn't beat.'

'Say it,' Harry said as he rattled the boy's shirtfront. 'Say it!'

'Yeah, like, I'm sorry that I caused the accident,' the boy mumbled.

'You'll be sorrier after I have a conversation with your father, kid.'

'So,' the policeman said, 'you admit you caused the accident, boy?'

'I confess,' the young man hurried to say. 'I did it.'

'You're not going to arrest him?' Faith objected.

'Him?' The policeman laughed. 'No, now I have this confession I *don't* arrest Mr Holson. He claims he was making a citizen's arrest and the boy resisted. Judge said one more assault and battery and I was to take Holson down to the police center and lock him up and throw away the key. But a confession—it clears everything. Definitely a citizen's arrest. Besides, you would be a character witness, *domina*?'

'Of course,' Faith replied. And then, *sotto voce*, 'He's a character, there's no doubt about it.'

'And now you all get out of my hospital,' Sister Robinson insisted. 'Very soon it is time for supper, and my patient should not be excited. Doctor's orders.'

She shooed them out of the room like a sheepdog clearing a paddock. All except Harry. 'Not me,' he insisted, and hung back until the others had all gone.

'Pull up a chair,' Faith invited. He complied, opening the venetian blinds as he went by. The last of the tropical daylight crowded in on them. 'Oh, my,' Faith murmured as she saw the damage to his face.

'He was bigger than I expected,' Harry said. He sat down heavily in the rickety bamboo chair. 'And I had to chase him all the way over to Fort Smith.'

'You really ought to control yourself,' Faith lectured. 'Leave it up to the law. I'm sure we don't need any vigilante trials on St Kitts.'

'My father always says that,' he admitted.

Faith shook her head and then immediately regretted it. Her mind began to spin like a top out of control. She lay back into the pillows and tried to concentrate on the ceiling. Of high white plaster, it was, with a web of tiny cracks. But it did give her a moment to settle her stomach. And her mind. Construction is a tough business, she reminded herself, and it breeds tough men. Which is why I turned to law. Besides, I don't know enough about him to judge. After all, *he* was in the cart as well as O'Malley and I. So maybe he's not being a White Knight. Maybe he did it for himself? If so, he operates on a very short fuse indeed!

She heard his chair scrape on the floor as he moved closer to the bedside. A moment later one of his hands surrounded both of hers and warmed them. There was no need for thermal warmth, of course, not on a tropical island like St Kitts. This was a warmth of the heart. And she enjoyed every calorie of it. Strange, she thought. I've only known him for a few hours, and I have this— treasuring already. I wonder what Ma Latimore would say?

'Head bother you?' A soothing, quiet question.

'I shouldn't have moved my head,' she said. 'The doctor says it's a small concussion, and I should be well enough to go back to the cottage tomorrow. Right now I feel better with my eyes closed.'

'It's always better to rest,' he said. And then there was a gap in the conversation. Her bed shifted subtly as he changed position. There was a warm breath that passed over her forehead, and a soft touch on the tip of her nose, as if she might have been feather-kissed. Her smile was irrepressible.

'That's better. That's my girl,' he murmured.

Which would have raised a very large number of questions in any girl's mind. 'Why did you do that?'

'Oh, it seemed the right thing to do.'

'And I'm *not* your girl. I'm not *anybody's* girl!'

'No need to get excited. It's just an old saying.'

'And you're an old sayer?'

'Time to change the subject,' he said ruefully. 'Did I tell you that my father came over from San Juan this afternoon?'

'No, you didn't. A planned trip?'

'Not exactly. He travels when he pleases.'

'Then perhaps you'd better run along to entertain him.'

He laughed as he got up from the chair. 'I do have to go,' he said, 'but it's strictly business. I did want to say that when you're ready to go home tomorrow I'd be glad to come for you.'

'You'd better stop off at the emergency-room,' she said, chuckling. He stretched, and from her position flat on her back he seemed to stretch up to the ceiling.

'None of that, now,' he teased. 'Nobody likes a smarty-pants.'

'You can't mean me,' she rejoined. 'I—don't seem to have any pants at all.' The blush started somewhere down around her left knee, and ran up through her hairline. She stifled it with another casual question. 'Why doesn't your father need entertaining?'

'Because he's been invited to stay at Rose Cottage with Lady Sunny,' he said. 'Cottage! With fifty rooms!'

'Fifty-six,' she corrected.

He bent over and deliberately kissed her forehead. 'I'll see you around.'

Yes, she thought, as she watched him leave, but be gentle. My head has a crack in it. I wonder if they have a cardiac section in the hospital? I seem to be having some sort of trouble with my heart as well!

Supper was not what she had expected. Slices of roast suckling-pig, chicken pilaf, and a vegetable plate consisting of platanoes, breadfruit, hearts of palm, and pawpaws and pineapple chunks. She was following it up with island coffee—half and half hot milk and strong black coffee—when O'Malley came strolling in. His grin told her everything she needed to know.

'You wouldn't believe, *domina*. Big. Big and blue. Plenty of room for me, plenty of room for milady. I take it for a ride out to the cottage, and introduce it to Isabelle. She knows right away she is retired, and it make her feel very good. So only the cart feels bad; nobody misses the cart. They got company at the villa. You know?'

'Company? Oh, lord, I forgot. Mr Holson?'

Mr Holson the elder, she reminded herself. Coming to spend the evening at the villa with Lady Sunny. And nobody else besides the sixteen maids and numberless housemen. And the seven cats. And the three guard dogs. And what was it that her instruction book said—in large print? 'Look out for elderly good-looking men, most of whom would like a share of milady's over-stuffed money purse.' And if only Mr Holson looked anything like his son, there was enough 'handsome' to go around the whole cottage.

'O'Malley,' she said sharply. 'I have to go home. Bring the car around at once.'

'At once, *domina*.' He looked at her as if she could do no wrong. But five minutes later the nurse was willing to argue, and twenty minutes later the night staff doctor came rumbling in, bound and determined to change her mind.

'Impossible,' he said for the fifth time. 'You have to be quiet.'

'I can be just as quiet at the villa as I can here,' she said very firmly. 'Here you have three people on duty. At the villa there are eight people on night duty, all well-trained.'

'If you rattle your head,' the doctor threatened, 'it's bound to fall off.'

'So I won't rattle my head,' she told him. 'But I *will* go!'

'I can't allow it,' he said. 'That's my final decision.'

'Have you ever been sued for malpractice?' Faith asked.

'I—you can't prove that! I am a careful, conservative doctor.'

'For your information, doctor, the villa maintains a staff of six lawyers. It is my bounden belief that they could prove that the earth is flat if they wanted to. Or would you prefer that I call Lady Sunny?'

'But that's not honest!'

'But it is realistic. Are you willing to take a chance?'

'No,' he said, sighing. 'I have a wife and children to support. So go home. I will write in the book "self-discharged". Don't wiggle the head. Keep calm. Don't be excited. I would wish that you live to be twenty-five.'

'Oh, I've already done that,' Faith Latimore said sweetly. 'You could perhaps have someone help me to the door?'

He shrugged his shoulders in a truly Gallic gesture in this most British of all islands. 'I don't understand. But go.'

'I don't understand it either,' Faith murmured under her breath. 'But as a well-trained lawyer I can smell danger at Rose Cottage.'

CHAPTER THREE

'WELL, what you think of that, Miss Faith?' O'Malley called from the spacious front seat of the stretch limousine. 'You don't like this color blue, the man says he could have it painted any shade blue you wish in twenty-four hours. Nice?'

'Nice,' Faith replied hesitantly, doing her best to hide the tremor in her voice. 'And big. Why so big?'

'Always for Lady Sunny,' he said as he reverently set the hand-brake. 'Always the biggest!'

'Yes. Yes, of course.' Faith flexed her wrist. She had been holding on to the side-bar of the back seat with all her strength since they'd pulled out of the hospital entrance. Whether it was the car or the driver she was not yet sure. Part of it was because everyone on St Kitts drove on the wrong side of the road. 'Of course,' she repeated hesitantly. 'Always the biggest makes the best. How much would you say it cost?'

'Cost?' He turned around and stared at her, flicking on the interior lights as he did so. 'Never think to ask, ma'am. Milady never worries what's to cost. She says if you gotta worry about cost you can't afford it.'

'No doubt,' Faith said, sighing.

'An' I am proud to drive you, Miss Faith. You sit so straight with the back, almost like the Queen, you know. Dignity! Keep the head straight, pose the arm to greet with the fingers—everything perfect!'

You bet, Faith told herself. Sit up straight because I'm afraid to relax, no? Keep the head straight or it falls off, no? Lord, I ache. All because I dare not leave milady alone in the house with this con artist. And his lovable son has bruised me up and down and sidewise—probably just to clear the decks for his father! I can't seem to get in balance with the Holson family. Why me, Lord?

'Ah. Here they come.'

'Here, who?'

The limousine had coasted to a gentle stop just at the foot of the ramp, and now two maids and a houseman were presenting themselves, pushing a wheelchair.

'And who arranged all this?' She shifted slightly forward in the deep-cushioned seat. 'And how?'

'I buy this car,' O'Malley said with some pride in his voice as he patted the steering-wheel, 'because it have a police radio, and entertainment radio, and a telephone radio.'

He held the last instrument up for her to admire. 'So when I see how much trouble Miss Faith have to get into the car down at the hospital I telephone Mr Napoleon to have—well, welcoming party. With chair, of course.'

'Yes, with chair, of course.' It all seemed so easy, Faith told herself wearily. Why can't I get a grip on things? James Bond had a submersible auto! I wonder if this one floats?

Somebody snatched the door open beside her. A tall, white-haired somebody, dressed in a formal white suit and black tie. Male. And a tiny goatee. Big. He might have been Tarzan's father. Or Colonel Sanders?

'*Domina*. Welcome home.' A deep, dark voice that rattled her already disturbed brain-case.

'Yes, I——'

'Of course, we haven't met.' A massive hand took her upper arm and seemed to lift her up out of the car. 'Holson,' he said, at somewhat a lower level than a hurricane. 'Nathan Hale Holson, at your service.'

'Yes, I met——'

'My son, Harry. Nice boy. His mother always liked him.'

She offered him a tentative smile as two of the maids assisted her into the wheelchair. His mother liked him—and you don't? she thought.

'The name is familiar, Mr Holson. Nathan——'

'Hale. In the American Revolution. An inept spy for General Washington. Yes. A collateral branch of the Holsons. "I have but one life to give for my country"? Something like that. When I was in the military we gave up that philosophy. We no longer seek to give up our lives for our country; now we encourage the enemy to give up *his* life for *his* country.' A brief cough, a look around the perimeter of the world, and, 'What a lovely night this is.'

And I am the *domina* of this household, which means I am in charge of everything and everybody in this villa—with the exception of Lady Sunny. Just what the devil are you doing here, without invitation or summons? she wondered silently. So, with a great deal more subtlety, she asked.

'Oh, Lady Sunny and I are long past the invitation stage. Ms Pearl always kept a room ready for me, you know.' His brilliant eyes caught at the blankness of her own, and he expanded his answer.

'Ms Pearl. The *domina* who preceded you in the position.'

'Yes, I know of Ms Pearl. And you have your own room here? And you just dropped in and——'

'And Lady Sunny invited me to dinner. Milady is changing at the moment. Do I detect a certain skepticism?'

The social Faith Latimore, loaded with manners and suspicions and construction knowledge, stepped on stage. 'Oh, no, not at all. It's just that Lady Sunny has a large number of interests, and until I know you better I feel it necessary to inquire. You're building that huge hotel complex, I understand. You must have millions of dollars tied up in that. I've been given to understand that builders always have money troubles.'

His eyes gleamed. 'Millions,' he confirmed. 'We're always scratching for money. Whatever happened to Isabelle?'

The change of direction spun Faith's damaged head around in circles. She fumbled for words.

'We were—involved in a small accident. Isabelle has been retired to pasture, and we have substituted this——' Faith waved a hand vaguely in the direction of the long blue auto, but she didn't quite know what to call the thing. 'So we purchased this small auto as replacement. I haven't had a chance to talk it over with Lady Sunny as yet.' Nor with your slick son, who, for all I know, might have set up the accident and the whole darn afternoon just to get a clear space for you to come calling, she added silently.

'Small auto? A sense of humor, my dear.' When he laughed his little goatee bobbed up and down. Faith stared at it, fascinated. 'Something that's been lacking for some years, humor. Let me give you a suggestion. Forget about talking it over with milady. The estate has needed an auto for years, and if you never bring the subject up with her she'll never know what you're talking about.'

'Until she rides in it,' Faith murmured.

'Lady Sunny has a tendency toward selective remembrance,' the big man said. 'Even after she rides in it, you can easily suggest it was something that Dicky ordered years ago, but the factories couldn't get it built soon enough.'

The entourage halted at the curve of the ramp, where the corridor to Faith's suite turned right. The corridor to the guest rooms, all twenty-six of them, turned left.

'You don't think that's a slight bit devious?' she asked as the houseman turned her chair. The smaller guiding wheels squeaked. Both maids giggled their embarrassment.

'The squeak would be more embarrassing than the auto,' the tall Texan called after her. 'Believe me.'

'Hurry,' Faith whispered to the houseman. There was so much she had to do. Change to an evening gown. Take four of those pills the doctor had prescribed—— And there was another one to keep an eye on. The good doctor. Young enough to fit into Lady Sunny's circle of friends. Whoever they were. And then back to the dining-room with her head tucked carefully under her arm to keep it from falling off! The wheels of the chair squeaked again. Faith winced. The old man was absolutely right. A squeaky wheel was much more out of place in Rose Cottage than any number of automobiles.

It seemed to take forever to get her to her suite. Up any number of ramps and through any number of halls but, finally, the houseman stopped at another of the ornately decorated doors and knocked. Mary, her maid, opened the door. 'Welcome back, Miss Faith. Will you be dining with milady and her guest tonight?'

Faith was pushed into the room. The slight jar as they crossed the threshold bounced her skull unmercifully. She took a minute to answer.

'Yes, I will.' Faith was striving not to nod her head, just in case it wasn't securely attached. 'But I think I'll need the wheelchair for at least one more day. I don't dare to take a chance.'

'Best thing,' Mary replied. 'You take a shower now? Maybe you have a glass of Irish coffee?'

While the maid went for the coffee, Faith relaxed in her wheelchair and looked around this amazing suite. It consisted of two rooms and a bath, each about three times as large as her bedroom at home in Massachusetts.

There were no corners. The walls merged into each other in graceful curves rather than angles. Soft buttercup walls that reflected the tropical sun and spread happiness around in all directions.

The mahogany and bamboo furniture was commodious, but the rooms contained it all with no trouble. The slip covers were silk brocade, embroidered with lovely flowers in a pale pink, pale yellow and palest lavender on a subdued green background. Faith had tried to describe the room to her mother in a letter written on the first day of her arrival, but had given it up because it all sounded so fantastic. The sweet, flowery scent of the bouganvillaea climbing the outer walls was an added bonus. It was the type of aroma one would wear as perfume. Come to think of it, Lady Sunny did.

As she looked around the room Faith noticed a computer terminal on her desk. It hadn't been there earlier. Faith was loaded with typical Irish curiosity. She carefully wheeled her chair over to the machine and flipped it on. The machine's menu listed its contents. Social notes, correspondence, finances—all neatly separated.

Mary came back in with her Irish coffee. 'I don't have the time to study the contents,' Faith said. 'Do you think I might let it print out some of its data?'

The woman smiled and threw up both her hands. 'I don't understand it from front to back. We have a machine-secretary, but she is off on vacation right this moment. You feel like turning on the switch, you goes right ahead, Miss Faith. Me, I stand back out of the way. How do you like——?'

Faith had just tried her first sip of the coffee, and came up choking half to death.

'—your coffee, ma'am?'

Faith managed to get her breathing tubes clear, and wiped her eyes. 'There's more than five per cent alcohol in that?' she demanded.

'Yes,' Mary said, chuckling.

'More than ten per cent?'

'I do believe so.'

'More than——'

'Even that,' Mary teased. 'Come on. We get you your shower now and get you dressed before dinner. It don't pay to be late for meals in Rose Cottage! What you like to wear tonight, Miss Faith?' She gestured at the north wall, which was fitted cabinets from side to side. And when she opened the door Faith took a deep breath.

'Yes,' she said. 'One of those and one of those and one—— Lord, how can I make a choice? Where did all this stuff come from, Mary?'

Mary shrugged and grinned again. 'The lawyers in London, they send most of it. The rest comes from Paris. Smart lawyers, Lady Sunny have. Which one you like? Dress, I mean, not lawyers.'

'You suppose they got the right sizes?'

'Guaranteed,' the maid laughed. 'Never make a mistake. And in this closet over here we have——'

'Don't open the door. Let me guess,' Faith commented. 'Shoes?'

'Shoes,' Mary confirmed. 'I think maybe you have seen this movie before?'

'Help me up,' Faith said. 'I can't laugh for crying. I need a shower.' The shower had been running for some time as Mary, dressed in a very practical bikini, and Faith, dressed in nothing at all, made their way into the room. A cloud of warm steam filled the room. Faith inhaled gratefully. The heat eased her muscles as she moved into the shower stall. Once again the heat relieved her pain. She moved gracefully under Mary's hands as soap and love were applied, and then it was over. She took the towel that Mary offered, dried her face and neck, and wrapped it around her waist.

'Sit,' the dark beauty commanded, offering a tall, rubber-tipped stool. 'We brush the hair. And dry you off.'

And what about that? Faith asked herself as she complied. Here I am with a thousand commands to offer, and everyone already has all the directions they need! But still, she felt the better for it all, and she gradually relaxed, leaning against Mary.

'What would the *domina* like to wear this evening?' Mary, the ever-helpful aide, was at her side escorting her out into the cool of the bedroom, where a selection of dinner gowns lay across the bed. Faith made a mistake. She turned her head to admire too quickly, and her world went into a spin.

'Something light, easy to get into and something I can wear sandals with,' Faith grumbled as soon as she had recovered her equilibrium. 'I think perhaps the gold lamé?'

'Delicious,' the maid responded, and held the gown up. Faith gulped. Of all the Latimore girls Faith was the one who suffered most from an overwhelming sense of modesty. The dress was magnificent in the front, and practically non-existent in the back, leaving no room for a bra or any other protective devices underneath.

'Oh, lord,' Faith groaned.

'Listen. If you've got it, flaunt it,' the very practical little maid returned. 'And you've got it!'

'Yes,' Faith muttered. 'But it's mixed company. How long do I get to *keep* it all, I wonder?'

Mary shrugged and held the dress out. Had it not been for the horrible noise from next door, Faith might well have rejected the gown, but the noise was there. The computer printer in the adjacent room was running wild, beeping for attention. The dress slipped out of Mary's hands; the wet towel slipped off Faith's hips.

'Paper,' Mary called, agitated, as she took a quick peek into the room. 'The machine paper is all on the floor, *domina*, and the machine-secretary is on vacation!'

Faith came to the door and surveyed the scene. 'And you couldn't fix it?'

Mary threw up her hands. 'No, *domina*. Only the machine-secretary can do this work.' She backed off, sidled past the computer and out into the sitting-room. 'I don't know even who to call, Miss Faith.' There was an edge of desperation in her voice. 'We have the union, and nothing must be changed!'

'Not to worry,' Faith assured her. There was plenty to worry about, but why spread it all over the villa? But neither could she leave things as they were. Computer beeps were among some of the most annoying sounds in the world to people who had aching heads. Faith took her courage in her hands and staggered out into the sitting-room to the rescue. The machine had piled up yards of fan-fold paper on the floor.

Refilling the paper bin was not too difficult. It required patience and a steady hand. And when the bin was topped off the printer started itself off again at full speed. Mary stared, astonished. No *domina* in her experience had ever been capable of such repair. What a story this would make in the servants' hall!

Faith savored the praise and then rested her weary head on her arms at the computer-station table to let the world settle down.

But the machine chuckling along beside her was soon out-noised by a loud voice in the hall. Faith stirred, looking for her lost towel. Mary was arguing with a man at the door of the suite. Faith opened one eye. Harry Holson stormed into her sitting-room.

'Damn you, Holson,' Faith groaned. She had nothing to hide behind. She picked up a massive armload of printed paper and constructed a fortress around herself to maintain her modesty.

'Was this the plan all along?' Harry asked sarcastically. 'You planned to use me as bait to trap my father? Well, let me tell you, it isn't going to work. No gold-digging little tramp—or even her gold-digging employer—is going to run my father into *that* trap!'

Faith was silent; she was concentrating on keeping covered. Harry continued. 'Aren't you even going to try and play the innocent with me? I've got you pegged, haven't I? What's it take to keep this mausoleum running? What—Lady Sunny running short of cash?'

Faith had reached her limit. So had the paper. It was falling off in certain strategic places, and sticking suggestively to other parts. She'd heard enough.

'What do you mean? We don't need your father's money! Why is he trying to latch on to Lady Sunny? Has business been in a slump lately? How much is he looking to recoup out of Lady Sunny? I've never met a construction man that didn't need more money! Why have you been lurking around? Casing the joint?'

Faith was so angry she was beginning to sputter. Her hands began to pull harder on the wet, perforated paper sheets behind which she was trying to hide. Needless to say, the paper gave up the battle and, suddenly, important parts of her anatomy were uncovered to the cool twilight air.

But anger, one of Faith's worst characteristics, was consuming her. How dared he accuse either her or milady of any underhand actions? The pot calling the kettle black? How dared he suggest that milady would need anyone's money! Or that she, Faith Latimore, wanted to get involved with a second-hand construction grunt! She'd grown up with them and, as a rule, they weren't her type. Her mother had married the only acceptable construction man of Faith's acquaintance. And God wasn't making any more models like Bruce Latimore!

'Get out of my room,' Faith shouted, and pointed dramatically in the direction of the door. It would have been a regal moment if the hand she'd pointed with hadn't been the hand holding the paper up, and if, immediately after pointing, that same hand hadn't gone to her forehead in an attempt to stop the pounding headache. At that moment the door opened again and Mary came in with two housemen at her heels. She took one look at the situation and scurried into the bedroom, coming out with a sheer bathrobe. She helped Faith into the robe and Faith repeated, 'Get out, Mr Holson. These gentlemen will show you the door. Please don't linger.' With that, she stalked gingerly toward the bedroom.

'This argument isn't finished,' Harry called after her. 'This is just the beginning. Remember, stay away from my father. And keep the lady away, too!' With his last threat given, he stomped out of the room, followed closely by the housemen.

'Mary?' Faith asked, forcing her eyes open. 'Has he left yet?'

'Yes, missy,' Mary said. 'Do you need some help to get back to the other room?'

'What makes you think that?' Faith said with a small, one-sided grin. 'I'm dressed to kill, aren't I?'

'Maybe we should drink a toast to the victory,' her maid suggested.

Both of them headed for the drinks cabinet.

Forty-five minutes later Mary wheeled Faith into the drawing-room. It had taken that long for Faith to get control of herself. For Mary to help her into the silky, full-length A-line dress of pale gold, the matching sandals—no nylons needed—and to help her put on the minimum amount of make-up Faith would wear. Mary, as far as Faith was concerned, was a helpmeet of major proportions. She was soon back in the wheelchair and headed out on to the ramp.

'Thank you, Mary,' Faith said. 'You've been a great help.'

'It's my pleasure, ma'am,' Mary said with a big grin. 'You bring much fun with you. You're going to shake this place up.' She turned them into the lounge and left her there, humming a little tune as she went.

'Are you?' a masculine voice boomed from her left shoulder.

'Am I what?' Faith asked. The senior Mr Holson stood by the bar with a drink in hand.

'Going to shake this place up?'

'I hope not.' Faith wheeled herself over to join him. 'As I remember, my contract with the London lawyers requires that I make no fuss. I would think that shaking things up would be classified as making a fuss. Wouldn't you?' She just couldn't help herself; she had to smile at him. Compared to his son he seemed so likeable. Dignified, charismatic, handsome. On the other hand his son was—sexy! Her face turned red, and she almost choked. 'What are you having to drink?'

'Bourbon and branch water,' Mr Holson said cheerfully. 'That is Bourbon whiskey and water to those of you from above the Mason Dixon line. Just to make sure I get the full effect of this wonderful sipping whiskey I don't add all that much branch water.'

'Very wise,' Faith said with a sad smile. 'I can understand why you would hold back from too much polluted water in your drink. It could be unhealthy.'

'You're so right my dear,' said Mr Holson. 'At my age, I must be careful of my health.'

They both laughed until Francis, the bartender, came back into the room with more ice and asked for her drink order. She ordered a Perrier water and then she and

Holson moved over to a small table at the side of the room. Francis brought her drink over to her and set it down carefully on the glass-topped table.

'How's your job going in Frigate Bay?' she asked. 'I heard that you've already got the foundation and the reinforced steel in place.'

'The job's going along well enough; I've got some small problems. It's nothing I can't take care of soon enough. The next step is the reinforcing beams, but we've got a wait on those.'

'Are you getting them from Henderson?' Faith asked.

'Yes,' Mr Holson said with a surprised look on his face. 'What do you know about Henderson?'

'I know that Henderson is having some production problems. I know that they're six months behind schedule and the orders are piling up.' How to look like an expert, Faith thought. Just listen to my father when he's having the same problems! Even Bruce Latimore loses his cool on occasions.

'How did you know that?' Mr Holson asked with real interest.

'I—er—know someone in the construction business,' Faith said with some pride.

'Are we talking Latimore as in Latimore Construction?' Holson elder inquired.

'Some relation,' Faith said cautiously, and took another sip of her drink.

'And you didn't follow in his footsteps?'

Faith took a deep breath. This wasn't time for a confession. 'No. My mother is a lawyer. I——'

'Ah. You followed your mother. Even split?'

'So to speak.' She clamped down on her tongue. There was no need to tell him that she found the law a gentler persuasion, where one did not have to compete with her sister Mattie or her young brother Michael, both brilliant driving minds. Both masterful managers. A tear twitched at her eye; she nudged it away. Why tell him there was no joy in being second-best?

They continued talking, mainly about the mistakes and foibles of construction and construction workers. They were one-upping each other in silly stories and Faith told him her favorite construction cartoon: Two men were holding a set of blueprints at the top of a *large* hole. One of the men yelled down to the foreman, who was at the bottom of the hole, 'Sorry, boss. We have the plans upside-down!'

Both of them were laughing when Lady Sunny came in, followed closely by Harry Holson, who looked immaculate in his beautiful white dinner jacket and Caribbean necktie. She hadn't seen him fully dressed before this. Her breath whistled down her throat and her eyes widened. She could see herself helping him take it off—the necktie, of course. Her pulse jumped until she forced herself to remember. She was here to ward off such pirates from Lady Sunny's bank account! Down, girl. Down!

She turned to Lady Sunny, who was coming across the floor; Napoleon followed with her glass of sherry. Milady was dressed, as usual, all in black. This evening it was a long black gown with jet trimming on the sleeves and neckline. She was wearing her diamond earrings—two carats each; her necklace—only the jeweler knew how many carats; and her large diamond ring—three carats, easy. But underneath the long, full-length skirt, Faith knew that milady was wearing a pair of light blue shoes studded with diamanté. Milady looked a lot like the end-of-an-era pictures of 1901 Queen Victoria, who also dressed in black. All that was missing was the lace head-covering.

'It's lovely to see all of you here for dinner but, *domina*, why didn't you stay in the hospital?' Lady Sunny asked as she reached the pair. 'I would have been

perfectly happy with Mr Holson, and I do worry about
you. I telephoned your dear mother an hour ago. She
says not to worry, for you have a very hard head. Did
you know that your grandmother and I were distantly
related? No, of course you couldn't know.'

'My mother is always right,' Faith replied, moving her
head gingerly.

'But of course. Mothers are always right. I regret that
Dicky and I had no children. None the less, I have called
the doctor to appear in the morning to give you a check-
up. My darling Dicky got a concussion once. He slipped
on the stairs—the next day we had them all removed and
replaced with ramps. It makes it so much easier for
wheelchairs and walking. Nathan, this is Faith Latimore,
my new *domina*. Faith, you've met Harry, Nathan's son,
already. Or so I've been led to believe?'

'Very true,' Harry responded from behind milady's
back. He stepped forward and extended a hand. Faith
swallowed her blush, ignored his hand, and backed her
chair away.

'We've been having a delightful chat,' the elder Holson
said. 'Your *domina* is distantly related to the most
famous construction company in the world. Bruce
Latimore gave us our start in the business. Sub-contracts.
And Miss Faith is a most discerning person in her own
right.'

'Thank you,' Faith murmured.

Milady held out her hand and Mr Holson bowed over
it, kissing the fingers. It looks like a French movie, Faith
told herself, but at least milady is accustomed to such
manners. As if she were peering through a veil of years,
Faith could see the older man's attraction. 'But not for
me,' she muttered under her breath. 'It's not what *I* want.

'I thought I asked you to leave,' Faith whispered
angrily to Harry, who was hovering over her wheelchair.

'Lady Sunny asked me to dinner,' he said, also in a whisper. 'I couldn't let the two of you gang up on my father. So hear me now—I'm going to be with you all night. I'm going to see that my father escapes you two sharks. Get used to me, lady. Think of me as a watchdog on patrol.'

'I'd really rather not think of you at all,' Faith responded. 'I don't understand how a perfectly lovely gentleman like your father could have sired such a small-minded man for a son. Tell me, how are you making out for finances this week? I understand some of your work is on the edge, so to speak.'

'Damn you,' he muttered. 'Who told you that?'

'Just a general observation,' Faith returned tartly.

'I suppose we're just lucky,' Harry said in a clipped, militant tone. 'We have more than enough for ourselves, just so we can keep other people's hands out of our pockets.' He smiled down at her with such an insincere look that it chilled her.

At that moment the dinner bell rang and the guests began to eddy toward the dining-room. Lady Sunny was escorted by Mr Holson and Faith was wheeled by Napoleon, with Harry walking beside her, still looking concerned—about her well-being? Or about her intentions? Lady Sunny was seated at the head of the table with Mr Holson on her right. Harry sat to her left and a space next to Harry was open for Faith. They sat and the dinner was brought out from the dumbwaiter. Consommé for starters, followed by curried Caribbean lobster served with peas in rice and asparagus. It all looked delicious, but Faith couldn't eat. Her headache wasn't going away and sitting too close to Harry Holson was providing no cure for her acidulous stomach.

While Faith sat and played with the food on her plate she overhead Lady Sunny and Mr Holson talking about the wine being served with dinner.

'Yes,' milady said graciously, 'my dear Dicky put down any number of bottles of good wine. I hope you're enjoying it. Dicky and I had such a good time traveling around Europe and the United States gathering just the right vintages for our wine cellar. Dicky was very skillful. They were wonderful days. I miss him constantly, you know.'

'But at least you have all those happy memories,' Nathan said consolingly.

'Yes, I do have plenty of those.' There was a moment of silence while she picked up her wine glass and offered a toast to Dicky. The company joined in.

'Our lady's memory is slipping,' Harry whispered to Faith. Since Faith had only that morning signed checks for the new consignment of wine, she refused to bite.

'Not so's I've noticed,' she whispered back.

Milady put her glass down gently. 'I understand you met the Declaur youngster today, Harry. He was never one of my favorite young people. His father was a nice boy, and his grandfather was a good friend and one of Dicky's companions, but the child—— I find it difficult to measure the younger generation...'

'Yes, ma'am,' Harry said in his Texas drawl, which seemed to get thicker when he was about to prevaricate. 'He ran into us on the way to Basseterre and he and I got together later. He came to the hospital to visit Ms Latimore with me. To console her on her injuries.'

Faith almost gagged on her glass with the new slant given to the whole incident. Luckily, milady took over the conversation and directed it back to friends she had around the island, and from there to fashion. Or rather, the deplorable fashion taste of the wife of one of Dicky's friends whose picture had appeared in a gossip paper with slightly less than a complete covering. When the subject ran out she turned to the elder Holson and said,

'How is the construction you're involved in doing? What exactly is it that you are building?'

'We have a contract from a major hotel firm to build in Frigate Bay, next to the golf course. I'm of the opinion that a large hotel on the island will improve the tourist trade considerably. It would certainly improve the situation by more than eight hundred first-class jobs. And you know what the influx of cash would do, Lady Sunny.'

'I'm not sure I want any more people on the island. But we certainly need jobs for our own people. I suppose you would know best. My Dicky was so intelligent about this sort of thing. He just wanted me to be happy. I'm happiest now if things remain the same.'

'Are you suffering at all from this global recession?' Harry asked milady.

'Harry!' Nathan said in a shocked tone. 'That's not a question that a gentleman asks a lady. I thought your mother and I had taught you better.'

Milady looked inquiringly at Faith as the holder of all information financial. 'The shoe business is doing splendidly,' Faith rushed to assure Lady Sunny, even though she didn't think the concept of cash shortage would ever cross milady's mind.

'Are *you* having any problems with the recession?' Faith asked Nathan Holson. What's sauce for the goose is sauce for the gander, she thought as she speared him with the question between courses. 'Is it causing problems with your project?'

'*Domina,*' Lady Sunny said sorrowfully. 'I had expected better of you.'

'It's all right, milady,' Nathan Holson said. 'It's just that I'm momentarily short of funds. In fact, if I don't get five million US dollars soon, I won't be able to finish this contract profitably.'

'Oh, my dear,' milady said with concern, 'I wouldn't want that to happen. It would be just too disappointing for you. Surely you have resources to get the money from a loan, don't you?'

'Please,' Mr Holson said reassuringly, 'I don't antici-pate any problems with getting a loan. In fact, it's pretty much in the bag, as we say in Texas.' He joined this last sentence with a hearty laugh in which everyone joined.

Faith's laughter was rather forced. Secretly she felt she was finally at the bottom of the well. So, she thought, the Holsons need money and the loan is in the bag? From whom? Banks? Or Lady Sunny? Sure, your loan is in the bag—as long as you don't have to face me for it! Not a penny, Mr Holson, not a red cent. I am going to beat you to the pass, cowboy! she vowed.

'Well, let me know if I can help,' Lady Sunny said. Faith almost choked on her wine.

'Got you there,' Harry murmured as he patted her back. She glared at him, still coughing.

The dinner party adjourned to the sitting-room where Lady Sunny kept her embroidery frame. The gentlemen had relaxed with glasses of the fine brandy Dicky had laid down. Milady started her needlepoint. By this time, Faith's headache had grown to major proportions, pounding against her skull like the surf at Palmetto Point.

'Please excuse me,' she said, 'But I think it's about time for me to go to my room. It's been a lovely evening, milady, gentlemen. I will bid you all goodnight.' She wheeled herself over to the door and it opened im-mediately. Mary waited outside to take her to her suite.

'*Domina* didn't eat much of her dinner,' Mary com-mented as they rolled up the ramp to the second floor of the house.

'What is this?' Faith grumbled. 'Is there an infor-mation line going through the house?'

'I was just in the kitchen after dinner and Cook noticed your plate,' Mary said reasonably. 'We were worried you

weren't feeling well. So I waited for you to come upstairs. You don't look too healthy, missy. You got any
more of those pills the doctor gave you? I tell you, I get
you in your bed and then I get you some more medicine.
That sound all right?'

'That sounds fine,' Faith whispered. She was talking
softly because sound of any sort was stabbing her behind
the eyes and she knew better than to try a nod.

Mary left her in the sitting-room of the suite while she
got the bed ready and Faith's bedclothes laid out. Faith
looked longingly at the computer and the remains of the
printout she'd asked for earlier. She knew that there was
no way she was going to be able to read any of it tonight.
But tomorrow——!

'Here we go,' Mary said as she came back into the
sitting-room. 'It's time for bed.' With Mary's help Faith
did finally slip between the soft linen sheets and when
she closed her eyes she was thinking hard about what
she could do to veto any of the Holsons' plans to get to
Lady Sunny and her uncounted millions. She was going
to have to count them, tomorrow!

CHAPTER FOUR

MORNING brought sunshine and the scent of bougain-
villaea through the window. Morning also brought the
doctor and his grumpy bedside manner through the door.

'How do you feel?' he asked gruffly as he listened to
her heartbeat and took her blood-pressure.

'Much better,' Faith said honestly.

'You'd feel even better if you'd stayed at the hospital,' he complained as he checked her eyes and ears.
'The only reason I'm here this morning is that I like my
job and Lady Sunny could make some serious problems
for me. So now that we know you'll live, I'm going back
to my hospital for rounds. Good day, *domina*.'

Faith grinned a crooked grin at him. Since last night
she had discovered that Lady Sunny sat on the hospital
board of governors. 'Stay for breakfast,' she invited,
knowing he wouldn't. He found excuses and ran.

When Mary came in Faith took a quick shower and
dressed in a cream-colored sundress. She pinned her hair
up off her neck and had Mary put sunscreen on her
shoulders and back. 'Ready for any dragons there be in
the house this morning,' she told the maid. 'Or, as my
father used to say, "loaded for bear".'

Mary smiled discreetly. She was coming to enjoy the
new *domina*, even if she didn't understand half of what
was going on. Things were happening at Rose Cottage.
Life was becoming interesting—most interesting.

'Have you seen either of the Holsons this morning?'

'Yes, Miss Faith. Mr Holson, the elder, he has gone
out with milady for a drive in the new car.'

'Damn!'

'You don't like if milady goes riding in the car?'

'I don't like if milady goes riding in the car with Mr Holson. How about the other one?'

'Mr Harry? I see him on the veranda having breakfast a minute ago.'

'You mean they both spent the night here?'

'Yes, they did,' Mary said. 'Both of them.'

Oh, boy, Faith thought, I'm running a hotel for rakes, when I ought to be running a nunnery. How in God's world can I keep milady's money in her own pockets? I think I need to run an education program for her before she turns Rose Cottage into a boarding-house!

And I had hoped to take her for her first auto ride, too, so I could explain about the car and the accident and Isabelle. Instead Lady Sunny is out cruising the highways with a shark and getting the word direct from the shark's mouth! Somehow or other things are more complex than they ought to be!

Faith grabbed her notebook and headed for the veranda. The housemen were spraying the lower ramps again, taking advantage of milady's absence. That's what I need, she told herself. A big can of beau repellent. Surely there must be something available on the market?

She found Harry sitting in a comfortable chair on the second-level veranda, above the level of the spray. He had a cup of coffee at his elbow, his nose deep in the local newspaper, and his feet up on the adjacent chair. He appeared to have moved in and taken over the household. How to get rid of him? The thought of dynamite crossed her mind, but Lady Sunny would be bound to notice the hole in the veranda floor—if any veranda were left.

'Good morning,' Faith grumbled. Harry looked up from the paper. 'I understand that your father and milady have gone out for a drive. Have they known each other long?'

'Yes,' Harry said. 'My mother and Lady Sunny were good friends and when she died milady was very good to Dad. They get along well. I think we could get along well too, if we tried.' He lifted his shoes from the other chair and sat up.

'It's only in the Bible that the lion lies down with the lamb.' She pulled out one of the chairs and a maid appeared almost as if by magic.

'Coffee, Miss Faith?'

'Yes. And Danish.'

'Wow! What a cheery person you are.'

'Drink your coffee and feel lucky,' she told him. 'I suppose now you're going to tell me that Lady Sunny invited you to stay over.'

He folded the paper neatly and set it aside. 'Got it in one.' He cocked his head slightly to get the sun out of his eyes. '"Because," she said, "*domina* always likes company at the breakfast-table and there's hardly anyone about." So here I am. About!'

'I should be so lucky!'

He leaned forward, elbows on the table. 'What is it with you? In twenty-four hours you've turned into the Grouch that ate St Louis.'

'What is it with me? Money,' she said. 'Lady Sunny's money.'

'Money? You think my dad is out to flim-flam the lady?'

'My very thoughts,' she returned. 'How about five million?'

'Five million? Chicken-feed.'

'Not if you haven't got it,' Faith insisted. 'And your father doesn't have it. He told me so last night at the dinner-table.'

'Well, I'll be damned!'

'Probably,' she replied, and turned to dip into the pastry plate that the maid had just placed on the table.

'What would you say if I told you we've already borrowed the money?'

'What would I say? Not a very polite word, to be sure. You have some proof?'

'As it happens, yes.' His jacket was slung over the back of his chair. He reached around and pulled out an envelope from its inside pocket. 'You'll forgive me if I take certain precautions,' he said as he took out the enclosed letter and arranged it so that she could only see the bottom half.

'Read, Thomasina.'

'Thomasina?'

'The feminine form of Doubting Thomas.'

Faith was torn in three directions. She could rage at his insult, slap his face, or try to puzzle out what the letter said. But a well-trained Latimore always had her eye on the main chance. In this case the last paragraph of the letter. 'And so we are happy to offer you a one-time guarantee on your loan of five million dollars at the percentage and terms of our previous guarantee.'

'Well!' Faith blushed and swallowed, prepared to eat a little humble pie. But there was something itching her memory. The guarantee number was in the code originally used by—— Her hand slipped, purely by accident, and knocked his thumb away from the top of the letter, and the imprint of the other company.

'Dear God,' she muttered. 'It's a forgery! My father wouldn't——'

'Ah, but he did,' Harry said, chuckling.

'I don't believe it. I'll have to call Michael.'

'Michael?'

'My brother Michael. He runs the Latimore Corporation.'

'Then I would propose,' he said, 'that we declare a truce until you have the opportunity to check it out.'

'Only as long,' Faith declared firmly, 'as we don't make accusations concerning money to each other.'

'We still have this bit to settle about your lovely Lady Sunny and *our* money,' Harry said. 'I don't see any income, and this "cottage" must cost a bundle to run.'

'This house *does* cost a bundle,' Faith stated. 'Lady Sunny's shoe factories make, and sell, three and a half million pairs of shoes a year!' Put that in your pipe and smoke it, Mr Holson, she added silently.

Harry was about to take another sip of the hot coffee. Something went wrong with his windpipe. He coughed and almost drowned himself. 'Three million?'

'And a half.'

'I—find that hard to believe,' he stammered. 'I'll have to check that out. In the meantime, I propose a truce. Bargain?'

'It's a deal,' Faith said as one of the maids brought out a second plate of pastries.

'Have some more coffee,' Harry offered. 'They make the damnedest coffee I've ever tasted around here.' He poured her a cup from the pot and passed it to her as she moved her seat into the shade. 'Do you want some of this newspaper? I like to keep track of what's happening.'

'I prefer my news orally,' Faith said. 'That way, it seems second-hand and not so threatening.' She paused to sip her coffee. It was bitter.

'*Café con leche*,' he told her as she made a face. 'Half coffee, half warm milk, and as much sugar as you can stand.' He fumbled among the pitchers on the table and rearranged things for her. She took another sip and smiled her gratitude.

There's really something nice about this man, her conscience told her. Something attractive! A girl my age could fit him into her life without half trying. If only his name were not Holson.

'Since you've read the paper, why don't you fill me in on the news?'

'Well,' Harry said, while watching her add two more teaspoons of sugar and a large dollop of cream to her coffee, 'evidently yesterday was a large day for vehicular accidents. Not only did our accident make the paper but over in Tabernacle a crate of chickens fell off a truck.'

'Oh, no,' Faith said with a concerned look. 'Is that considered a serious vehicular accident?'

'Yes,' he replied. 'Especially from the chickens' point of view. There was a bus following the truck. It ran over everything. Caused a big uproar in town, but they settled it in typical St Kitts fashion.'

'And what is that, may I ask?'

'Simple. They declared a holiday and everyone went along to the traffic court.'

'Was there anything else?' Faith asked as she looked over the pastry selections.

'There did seem to be some problems involving the US Coastguard and a suspected drug-smuggler last night,' Harry said as he looked over the story in the paper.

'Where?'

'At sea between St Croix and St Kitts,' Harry read. 'A few young people were evidently trying to import some recreational drugs for the tourists.'

'Why would that make the local paper?' Faith was curious.

'They were using a boat that was made in St Kitts. It sank.'

'It's a heart-warming story, no doubt,' Faith said after swallowing her mouthful of strawberry Danish. 'But I still don't understand why it would get print-space in the *St Kitts Gazette*.'

'One of the smugglers is a hometown boy,' Harry explained. 'The paper goes out of its way to print anything having to do with residents of the island.'

'I suppose,' Faith said hesitantly, 'that's a way to insure circulation. But, now that we've covered the news, does this paper carry the important stuff?'

'What are you talking about?' Harry smiled as he asked.

'The important stuff,' Faith said as she eyed the last Danish on the dish and decided to forgo the pleasure. 'The comics, the horoscope section and the sports news. I want to know how the Red Sox are doing! You know, the important news.'

'Why would you need to see the Red Sox in print? You know they're in last place, unlike the Texas Rangers.'

'Oh, please,' Faith said indignantly. 'I really don't care what position they are in just as long as they're ahead of the Toronto Blue Jays! As for the Texas Rangers, I thought that was what you called your State Police. Wasn't the Lone Ranger one of them?'

'We have a winning team,' Harry said, 'carrying on the best tradition of all Texans.'

'Yeah, yeah,' Faith said. 'But you guys feel that the Alamo was a win for the home team. It seems to me that they got whopped by a team from Mexico.'

'I have to warn you right now,' Harry said, trying to keep a straight face, 'that bad-mouthing Texans, Texas and the Alamo could end up costing you. I fully expect the heavens to open and lightning to strike you dead for deriding our famous and glorious history! Besides, don't you have a Texan brother-in-law? Didn't he teach you better?'

They might have continued this squabble for hours, but milady and Nathan Holson came out on to the veranda at that moment. Milady's cheeks were red from

the exertion. She looked one hundred per cent better
than she had the day before.

'Well, my dear,' Lady Sunny said to Faith, 'Dicky
made a wonderful choice. That car is magnificent.'

'Yes,' Faith murmured. 'He made a wonderful choice.
As we would expect!'

'You see, Nathan, how my *domina* agrees with me?
Dicky would have loved her.'

Nathan reached over Faith's shoulder and took the
last pastry from the platter. 'It's a beautiful day. Much
too nice to waste. Why don't you two young people go
for a ride around the island? Maybe you could take a
picnic.'

'That's an excellent idea, Nathan,' milady chorused
in agreement. 'You two should get out and see the sights.
I know that the *domina* hasn't seen that much of our
island. Why don't you go up to Fort Brimstone? They
have a lovely view from there. Dicky and I wanted to
build Rose Cottage on Brimstone Hill but the
government was against the whole idea. However, once
we saw this site we loved it.' Milady got a far-away, re-
membering look on her face. 'But I digress, my dears.
Today is a lovely day, you are both young, and it's not
supposed to rain until this afternoon. So take advantage
of the day. I'll arrange for Cook to prepare a picnic
basket.'

'But,' Faith protested, 'I have a week's worth of papers
and bills to take care of. And several purchases to review,
and——' But by that time Lady Sunny had smiled
vaguely, taken Nathan's arm, and walked away.

'Well, *I* didn't say anything,' Harry said apologetically.

'No, but you were thinking heavily,' Faith snapped.
'It's the last thing in the world I wanted to do, to go
picnicking with you!'

'Tut-tut,' he said. 'Lady Sunny has spoken.'

'You'd be some awful pain around the house, Mr Holson. I'll have to go change my shoes.'

'Out of three million pairs?' he suggested coyly.

'And a half,' she insisted as she snatched up her notebook and headed for her room.

'Thank you, Mary,' Faith said as she sat down on the chair and put on the pair of light, cream-colored socks that matched the low-cut walking shoes Mary had taken out of the shoe closet.

'Is no problem, missy,' Mary said cheerfully.

'Mary?' A startling thought had just struck Faith's mind. Go off alone with that man! Bull hockey!

'Missy?'

'How would you like to do me a great favor?'

'I would be pleased, Miss Faith. What favor?'

'Milady has *ordered* me to take Mr Holson on a picnic. I need a——'

'Chaperon?' Mary giggled.

'Exactly. A chaperon. Or a deputy sheriff.'

'I will run get my shawl, *domina*.'

The pair of them left the suite in anticipation and skipped down the ramp to join the others who were standing at the front door.

'Be careful, my dear,' Lady Sunny admonished. 'Don't overdo anything. The doctor gave you a clean bill of health but your accident was only yesterday.' There was a speculative look in milady's eye which indicated she was trying to remember what she'd planned to say.

'Oh, yes. Wear a hat! We don't want sunstroke as well as a concussion. Now, off you go, both of you. Have a good time.'

O'Malley had the car purring, waiting at the end of the ramp. The driver gave Mary a big smile as she climbed into the front seat beside him. As the car pulled away from Rose Cottage, Faith looked back and saw milady and Nathan Holson shaking hands.

'I wonder what that meant?' she murmured.

Harry squirmed around and looked out the rear window. 'I'm afraid I don't really want to know,' he said.

The interior of the car was as luxurious as she'd remembered from the previous day. 'Plenty of leg-room, Mr Holson?'

'Harry,' he insisted. 'Harry. We're operating under a peace treaty. Care for a drink?'

'Orange juice, please. Mary?'

'Nothing, *domina*. Thank you.'

'Very popular lady to take out,' O'Malley contributed. 'Not expensive. And still have a good time.'

'What are you thinking about?' Harry asked in a low voice.

'Nothing much,' Faith said, suddenly searching for something to say. 'Where are we going?'

'Brimstone Fort,' he said. 'About five miles from the cottage. In the 1700s it was the main defensive post on the island. A major tourist spot these days.'

'But no longer?'

'No longer, my dear. Times change. No more French invaders, no more pirates——'

'But plenty smugglers, drugs, revolutionaries, like that,' O'Malley contributed as he slowed the car and moved to the low-speed lane.

'I don't see a hill,' Faith commented as she looked around her.

'No, *domina*,' Mary said. 'This isn't Brimstone Hill, this is Half Way Tree.'

'Oh?' And does that sound as ignorant as I feel? Faith asked herself.

Harry chuckled. 'Back in the 1630s the French and the English shared the island,' he said. 'That tamarind tree over there was the boundary between the two, until England took over the entire affair. The tree is still flourishing. And that, up ahead, is Brimstone Fort!'

The car moved on and about two minutes later she could see Brimstone Hill and the scattered stones and demounted smooth-bore cannons of its defense. O'Malley pulled over on to a winding road that seemed to climb almost to the top of the hill. The parking lot about half way up gave access to stairs leading up to the ruins of the fort.

'Come on,' Harry said as he opened his door and stepped out of the car. He reached his hand in to help her out and when she caught it she felt a sudden electrical shock. She looked up at him, startled, as he climbed up the stairs ahead of her. His face was as changeless as forever. It hadn't meant a thing to him.

Oh, well, she told herself, and shrugged. Mary came around the car and handed Faith a straw hat. 'Please, *domina*,' Mary said. 'Milady did ask you to wear a hat when you're in the sun.'

Faith, who hated to wear hats, put it on and tied the blue ribbon under her chin. The sun was hot and very, very bright. Hats made sense.

It was only a short climb to the smooth grass of the top. The world seemed to stretch all around them. Both sides of St Kitts, an island to their north and the snow-crowned top of Nevis to the south were all visible. 'That isn't snow,' Harry explained, pointing to the top of the mountains on the neighboring island. 'Although that's what Columbus thought when he landed here.'

He reached down and took her hand. There's definitely a shock, Faith told herself. Definitely. She stole a quick peek from under the brim of her hat. He *had* felt something!

'Why don't we sit down?' he suggested. 'This used to be the commander's quarters. All gone now, of course.'

'How in the world do you know all this?'

'I make it a point,' Harry said as he bent down to look directly into her eyes, 'to get as much information as possible about whatever takes my fancy. Like you.' He whispered that last sentence and followed it with a soft kiss to her cheek. 'You smell like frangipani and your skin is as soft as a baby's, and you take my fancy!'

Faith froze, but then she shook herself and broke away from him. Find another subject, her brain roared at her. She took another step or two away from him. 'Is anyone else hungry?' she asked. 'I don't think that Danish I had for breakfast is going to hold me much longer.'

'I brought the basket, Miss Faith,' O'Malley said. 'Where you want to eat?'

Mary directed the operation, spreading the picnic cloth down on a pair of the larger granite stones. But to Faith's consternation the girl set places for only two.

'Aren't you two going to eat with us?' she asked.

'Oh, no, missy,' Mary answered. 'O'Malley and I have been walking out for two years now. We're going to sit over there with our sandwiches and Thermos. Have a good time.'

The contents of the basket were not the normal picnic items Faith was familiar with from home. There was sliced game hen, sliced ham, crab packed in ice, and several large, crusty rolls for sandwich makings. The cook had prepared a fruit salad of pineapple, bananas, strawberries and kiwi. There was a bottle of wine to go with the meal—a lovely, soft white Chablis from the French islands. Everything looked delicious and tasted even better.

Halfway through the meal Faith was struck by a sudden suspicion. 'Does this look like the sort of picnic a cook could pop together on a minute's notice?'

'Please,' Harry asked, around a mouthful of roll and game hen, 'don't try to take away my appetite. This food is too good to question and I'm hungry.'

'But doesn't it make you suspicious?'

Harry glared at her and opened the wine bottle. But Faith had been in the matrimonial hunt for too long to take it all serenely. One father and three sisters all trying to marry her off had left a predatory smell to it all. But the food *was* good. And when the last of the wine was poured and both Faith and Harry had done their best with the food, there was little or no talking. That was, if you didn't count 'please pass the salt' or 'don't you dare take that last piece of crab'.

They had eaten while seated on the benches by the granite slabs and when they'd finished Faith and Harry both got up slowly. 'If I'd sat there any longer,' Faith said, 'I think I'd have bonded to the seat. I've got to do some walking. Could we?'

Mary and O'Malley, who had been over looking at the islands in the distance, came back and started to clean up the picnic debris and pack the basket with all the leftovers. There wasn't much.

'If you look over to the east,' Harry said as he pointed in that direction, 'you can see St Barts and St Martin.' They walked around the cannon emplacements and Harry pointed again. 'This is north and those islands in the distance are Saba and Statia. That way——' Harry started as he turned, but Faith turned also and they were suddenly face to face. Harry looked terribly strained. He snatched at her, drawing her into his arms, and leaned slowly down toward her upturned face.

Oh, lord, Faith told herself, he's going to kiss me.

And he did.

It was a spectacular kiss, in Faith's opinion. It fulfilled the requirements she'd read about once on how to judge kisses. It had time, purity, and technique. And it was so impressive that she swore she felt the earth move. They parted slowly. Harry had a confused look on his face.

'I know that I probably shouldn't ask this,' he said hesitantly, 'but did the ground just shake for you?'

'Yes,' Faith said, still confused from the kiss and her reaction to it. 'Yes, it did. It did. Did it for you?'

Harry looked embarrassed and pointed over to the south-east. 'Those islands you see over there are Montserrat and——'

Faith obediently looked in the direction to which he was pointing. 'Is there an active volcano over there?' she asked.

'No,' Harry said. He was suddenly aware of the plume of black smoke that was rising from the south-east corner of St Kitts.

Somehow or another, Faith swore that she heard a telephone ringing. Or perhaps it was just a ringing in her ears. Five minutes later O'Malley came up from the car where he had been storing picnic leftovers. He waved in the direction of the thick plume of black smoke.

'Mr Harry, *domina*. Mr Nathan just called on the telephone.' The normally gentle driver looked as if he didn't believe the message he was bringing. 'He said that the smoke over there is a bomb that just blew up in your new building at Frigate Bay. He wants you to go and——'

In the car Harry took the cellular phone and started to dial. 'This is Holson. What happened?' There was a moment of listening and Harry said, 'How many are missing? Oh, my God! Any idea who did this?' The look on his face was grim.

O'Malley, who had been driving sedately, waited for no instructions at all. He put his foot to the floor and the big car began to move down the South Coast Road at high speed. Within minutes they passed Rose Cottage and headed for Basseterre.

As they came to the capital the sirens began to wail. The streets were congested with emergency vehicles. Traffic blocks were everywhere. O'Malley slowed the car, and every time he came to a policeman and a stopping point he leaned out the driver's window and yelled, 'Lady Sunny.' At which they were waved on.

Frigate Bay lay in the narrow neck of land that connected the Great Salt Pond to the main island, some two miles from the outskirts of Basseterre. The golf course was completed. The outline of two hotel towers climbed into the sky. An oily black smoke crowned the eastern tower. A police car waved them down just off the first tee.

'Mr Holson? Inspector Wheeler here. Four men are reported missing. Six are injured. We have begun evacuation of the injured, but there is a shortage of ambulances and nurses.'

'Give me that telephone, O'Malley. Inspector, this back seat is double width. You can use it as an ambulance.'

'And I am a qualified nurse,' Mary said. 'I stay with the car?'

'Yes.'

Faith stepped back out of the way. It was no place for a lawyer, no place at all. But it was...enlightening to see how Harry Holson stepped in and took charge. His fingers were busy at the cellular telephone, now working off its battery pack.

'Golden Rock Airport? This is Mr Holson, of Holson Construction. We have two helicopters on the ready line. I want them both at Frigate Bay golf course to transfer injured men to hospital. When? Right now, of course. Move it.'

And then he turned to the police inspector. 'You and your men will co-ordinate the flights?' The officer nodded. 'Now, where do you suppose my construction foreman is located?'

'Over by that shack in the middle of the area.' The Inspector gestured. 'What do you intend?'

'My people are best qualified to search the construction area,' Harry said briefly. 'I'll use this telephone to communicate with you, and you'll keep me posted?'

'Yes. Yes, of course.'

And what else could the inspector say? Faith asked herself. Men were curious creatures. One commanded, others obeyed. But wasn't it nice to be standing next to the man in charge? Subconsciously her hand slipped into his. He looked down, startled for a moment, then gave it a little squeeze. 'And as for you,' he said, 'you stick with me. I might need a good lawyer before the day is out.'

Faith meant to do just that. Stick with him, that was. She clutched at his hand with both of hers, defying the world to separate them. And then the noise hit her. The clash of sirens and engines, the pounding of the surf, the screech of the excited birds. It was the first time in her short life on the island that she had heard anything but the soft sing-song voices of people talking, the quiet sounds of the shore birds, or the deep, steady voice of the ocean. This was chaos! But then again, it wasn't, was it? With one masterful stroke Harry Holson had taken everything in hand, and there was order being impressed on to disorder. She squeezed his hand again as he towed her across the putting-green toward the construction shack, where the foreman and a pair of his men were waiting.

CHAPTER FIVE

IT WAS an hour after midnight. The onshore wind, flavored with smoke and soot, was gradually dying down.

'Let's go down to the beach,' Harry said to an exhausted Faith. 'There's nothing more we can do. The fire department has the fire under control. They've found all the missing personnel, and Dad is going to notify the families.' He took a deep, stretching breath and settled back down on his heels. 'We can rinse some of the grime off in the ocean.'

'I'm with you, bwana,' Faith said with a tired little smile and a faint attempt at humor. 'Lead the way.'

'Just down this hill,' Harry said as he led her down the green slope of the golf course toward the sounds of surf on the black sand. 'God! I'm tired.'

'You should be,' Faith said as she slipped her arm around his waist. 'You worked as if the devil himself were on your heels.'

'He was,' he told her. 'I felt as guilty as sin. Whatever happened was my fault.' He shook his head and squeezed her gently. 'You didn't do too bad yourself, kid. Organizing that outdoor feeding station was a life-saver.' Another pause. Faith looked up at his face, turned toward the moon. There was a runnel of—tears?—running down his cheek.

'I still don't understand. We've found all of our men alive, and yet there are two bodies in the wreckage,' he said. He pulled them to a stop. The moon was high, and the path they followed was paved with crushed white shells that gleamed in the early light.

'I'm glad Dad is here,' Harry said. 'I'm not much for handling the finer details. He can tell the families of the injured better than I can.'

He hesitated as they reached the edge of the sandy beach. They took off their shoes and socks, leaving them huddled in a little pile at the edge of the sand. With arms around each other—for comfort—they went on down the beach into the crashing surf.

Faith stopped when they were about knee-deep and turned to walk parallel to the shore. Knee-deep for her, of course, but hardly that for him. Arms around each other, they stood and let the ocean pound at them.

'So why would anyone blow up your site? Did you get any warnings or threats?' Faith asked.

'No!' Harry said forcefully. 'Nothing! Compared to some places this is an island paradise. There aren't any labor troubles, no strong left-wing elements, no international connections. I just don't know. All I'm sure of is that I'm responsible for these men.'

'There's nothing you can blame yourself for,' Faith said reasonably. 'Who expects crazies under the palm trees?'

'Still,' Harry said, 'I should have had more security. Or something! Something to protect the men that work for me! I'm responsible!'

'Harry Holson.' Faith stopped and looked him straight in the eye. 'As hard as it might sound, you can't protect everybody from the homicidal maniacs of the world. You do, and did, have security on the site. How much more could you have done? Your people have as much chance of being killed in a car accident, or a plane crash, or by a next-door neighbor with a shotgun and a bottle of whiskey. All your people are adults, and adults all take chances just by living. You have absolutely nothing to blame yourself for. Do you understand me?' If she hadn't been knee-deep in water she would have stamped her foot.

Harry was silent for a few moments, gazing up at the brilliant moon. Suddenly he grabbed her around the waist with both arms and drew her into a hard embrace. They held that position for a long, unbalanced moment, lips bonded to each other, struggling to stand against the increasing assault of the waves.

'Are you trying to take over control of my mind?' Harry asked between kisses.

'Huh.' Faith was not terribly coherent at this point. 'A likely story.' And she needed not another word. The waves increased at every swell; the next was the proverbial seventh wave. It knocked Faith off her feet, and Harry came with her. Down they went together, and then were rolled up the beach, thoroughly intertwined. They came up soaked, and laughing. As the wave receded their lips made contact again. Fire ran up and down Faith's spine. Fire and madness and hunger. All her disputes were put aside.

They broke apart to catch a breath. He held her two inches or more away from him as he brushed her hair off her face. 'Thank you,' Harry said, barely loud enough to be heard over the waves.

'Thank you,' she returned breathlessly.

'Thank me? You taste like salt-water taffy. Thank me for what?'

'You taste like heaven,' she told him.

'You might not be able to cure all my guilt feelings, but you certainly have helped. If you weren't here I'd probably be out trying to do something terribly macho. Like tracking down those saboteurs and hanging them from a tree.'

'You guys from Texas,' Faith said. 'You sound as if you're all in a *very* bad western novel.' She put her hands on her hips and glared at him. I've felt the same about

these people, she admitted to herself, but I'm not going
to admit it to Harry!

'The police will be working very hard on this case,'
she told him. 'I'm sure they'll be able to solve it. I mean,
how far away can the bombers get? It's a fairly small
island. There are only so many boats available. The
airport can be sealed off easily. Don't fret. The police
will get them.'

They rolled over a couple of times in the sand, teasing
each other, and after getting themselves thoroughly
sanded, struggled to their feet. They brushed themselves
off and started to walk back up on to the golf course,
in a far better humor than they had been earlier.

'That last one you pulled out,' Faith mused. 'The girl
that was stuck underneath that little car. Whatever happened to her?'

'I don't know,' he admitted. 'Once I passed her out
to you and the firemen I went to look for others. What
did you do with her?'

'I don't know,' Faith said. 'There wasn't any fireman
there, and when I pushed her all the way out from under
the building she just—disappeared.'

'I don't know. Probably somebody else got a grip on
her.' A moment later, walking hand in hand, he pulled
her to a stop. 'Isn't that funny? There weren't any other
women in that area except you.'

'Somebody will find her.'

'Yeah,' Harry said. He looked up and saw a Jeep
cresting the hill of the golf course. The hint of a new
dawning improved his sight. The bright chrome on the
sides of the vehicle identified it. Only the police used
that much sparkle and smarts.

'We'll find out something,' Harry told her. 'That's
Inspector Wheeler driving the Jeep. And headed right
in our direction.'

'I wanted to make sure,' the inspector said in his best public school accent a couple of minutes later, 'that we've accounted for all of your missing people.'

'What do you mean?' Harry asked. 'We had four men missing and we found all four. My foreman has accounted for all the men on the job site at the time of the blast. But there seem to be a couple of leftovers—a couple of extra bodies. Is something else wrong?'

'Yes,' the inspector said. 'We've found another body. A young man, apparently a native. Under the wreckage of a car. There's no doubt it was a car bomb and one of the drivers was too close to the explosion when it went off.'

'Any idea who?' Harry was quick to ask.

'Not at this time,' the inspector said. 'But we'll find out who it is soon enough.' With that clipped pronouncement, the police inspector turned his Jeep around and went back up the golf course slope toward the searchlights, the smoking remains of the eastern tower, and its underground parking garage.

Faith and Harry looked at each other and wordlessly decided to stay on the beach, away from all the destruction. They lowered themselves on to the soft grass at the edge of the green and relaxed. Shore birds were launching clumsily, making their way along the coast looking for breakfast. The gulls were already at sea, following the little fishing fleet out into the fish runs.

They listened to the hypnotic beat of the tide crashing on to the shore. They sat entranced as the beauty of another morning dawned in front of their weary eyes.

Faith fell asleep. She was awake one second and the next she was asleep, leaning against Harry's shoulder.

Harry suddenly felt her body go limp against his and looked down at her sleeping face. 'This has got to be uncomfortable, Faith,' he whispered. 'Let's get more comfortable so we both can sleep.' He laid her back

against the soft grass and joined her there, holding her
tenderly in his arms. This is one hell of a woman, he
thought just before he fell asleep. How did I get so lucky?

Faith was very comfortable. She didn't know what woke
her; she didn't really want to find out either. There. There
it was. That sound. What was that sound?

She opened her eyes and found herself sleeping spoon-
fashion with Harry on the outside. His arms were
comfortably around her. Except for the hand that rested
on her breast. It might have been a comfort to her while
she slept, but now that she was restored to consciousness
it was doing curious things to her psyche.

The sound was repeated again. Faith got up carefully,
slipping out of Harry's arms with a practised ease she
hadn't known she possessed. She was reluctant to do it,
but that sound was driving her crazy!

The mewing sound was coming from the west, in the
direction of several six-foot sand-dunes. Faith scrambled
toward the repeated sound. The dunes made things difficult. As she moved cautiously the noise resolved itself;
someone was crying. She had gone about a hundred feet
when she lost her footing and slid down the side of the
dune. At the bottom of the declivity a little lump of hu-
manity was trying to crawl up toward her.

The woman was covered with blackened dried blood
from cuts on her head. She had more blacking from
smoke, and looked as if she'd walked through fire and
had tripped a thousand times. She was dragging her left
foot as if it was damaged.

'Please,' Faith said as she wrapped her arms around
the broken body, 'let me help you. Sit down here and
I'll go wake up Harry. He'll get medical help for you.
Don't try to move more than you have to. Moving won't
help. I won't hurt you. I'll just go get help for you.'

Faith laid the woman down and ran back to where Harry was still sleeping. She knelt down and shook him awake. When he opened his eyes, he could see that she was upset about something. He sat up quickly.

'Harry,' Faith said, 'go up to the site and find a doctor. I've found someone who's been hurt badly. She needs medical attention. Please hurry.'

He was up quickly, taking a moment to make sure Faith herself was all right. He ran up the hill almost before his legs were under him. Faith ran back to the injured woman.

'Don't worry,' she told the woman, who had stopped trying to crawl away. 'Harry is bringing help. You'll be under medical care soon enough.' She knelt by the woman and took her hand, which seemed to be the only part of her not burned, cut or broken. The woman squeezed her hand and Faith kept on talking. She talked about anything. Faith never remembered what she said; she just kept talking to let the woman know she wasn't alone. Babbling it must have been, but she couldn't help herself. She wished she were her sister Becky, the doctor, who knew how to take care of this sort of trouble. But Becky was far away, in Massachusetts.

'Faith! Faith!' she could hear Harry yell after what seemed to be a small eternity. 'Where are you?'

'I'm here,' Faith called as she let go of the woman's hand and stood up. She could see that Harry had brought the police emergency medical team with him.

They came and took over very professionally. 'Ah, that one,' the police sergeant said as the team administered first aid and gently placed the girl on a stretcher. 'We've been searching the grounds for her for hours.'

The only thing that bothered Faith was that they were not very comforting to the patient. They were, in fact, downright cold to the woman. Faith was accustomed to the personal and comforting touch with which her sister and brother-in-law practiced medicine. However, the police soon had the woman up on the stretcher with an IV hooked up and the head bandaged to stop the bleeding.

'Is it bad?' Faith asked anxiously.

'All head wounds look bad and bleed tremendously,' the sergeant told her. 'I don't know about her leg. Maybe it's her hip. But we'll get this one up the helicopter pad, and very soon she'll be in good hands.'

They carried their patient up the hill, with Faith and Harry following slowly behind. At the construction site the stretcher was carried to the waiting helicopter. In seconds the giant bird roared into action, and once again the area was quiet.

Faith could smell the coffee, American style this time, coming from the canteen. 'I'll go get us some coffee,' she said to Harry.

'Good idea,' Harry said. 'Why don't you find us a table and we can eat whatever breakfast there is left? I want to go speak to the inspector right now. I'll be back in a minute.' He kissed her tenderly and then walked away.

'Well,' Faith muttered to herself, 'Mr Macho himself. That boy has seen too many Westerns. Kiss the woman and send her in for coffee. Let the big mad male star go and take charge of the situation. Who does he think he is—John Wayne?' Still muttering to herself, Faith moved into the canteen, procured two cups of coffee, and found a table for the two of them. She didn't notice the looks she was getting from the other inhabitants of the Red Cross shelter. She was too concerned about her latest patient—and, come to think of it, about Harry's dictatorial approach to the world. But at this moment she was too tired to *do* anything. Faith Latimore was *not* a morning person. She thought that people who were cheerful in the morning should be shot and put out of their misery. Nobody deserved to be happy before the noon hour.

Outside the canteen, Harry walked up to the inspector. 'Is your emergency medical team always so abrupt with their patients?'

'I beg your pardon?' Inspector Wheeler asked. 'Whatever do you mean?'

'They treated the woman Ms Latimore found,' Harry said, 'as if she were a criminal. They were efficient, but believe me they were cold.'

'Of course they were, Mr Holson,' the inspector said. 'They *were* treating a criminal. Who do you think drove that car into the parking garage? She did. We found her purse in the debris but we couldn't find her. She's one lucky lady to have survived. Thanks to you we now have her in custody.' With that, he turned and walked away towards his Jeep.

'Well,' Faith said just a touch testily as he joined her at the table in the canteen, 'what did you find out from the inspector?'

'I found out that the young woman you found was one of the drivers of the car bomb,' Harry said defensively. 'What else could I find out? And why are you angry with me? I thought we had that all settled.'

'I'm sorry,' Faith said. Suddenly she'd found her sense of humor. 'I'm not a morning person. I could get grouchy with Mother Theresa if she got to me before my second cup of coffee.' She took another sip from her coffee-mug. 'So, now we have an alleged perpetrator and, perhaps, a link to whoever is behind this atrocity?'

'God, I hate it when you speak lawyerese,' Harry said as he emptied his coffee-mug.

Faith managed to hitch a ride with the emergency crew from the Stone Fort Estate back to Rose Cottage. She was stiff in all her joints, and artfully painted up with smoke. Mary was waiting for her.

'A quick shower,' the maid informed her. 'Milady is waiting on the veranda. She wishes to breakfast with you.'

'Oh, lord,' Faith groaned. 'Have I let everything in the cottage go to pot? Hustle me into the shower, Mary. I'll bet I've blown my high-caliber job up over the moon.'

'Not to worry,' her maid told her as they walked toward the shower. 'Last person got fired at Rose Cottage was fourteen years ago. He made some foolish statement about how ugly Lady Sunny's blue shoes were.'

'Yes, I could see how that would be a suicide statement,' Faith said. 'And don't forget to lay out my blue diamanté shoes, right?'

Lady Sunny was having a conversation with one of the maids, and was sitting cozily with her at a small round table on the veranda. Milady was dressed in her usual black silk, down to her ankles, with a large square neckline, for coolness' sake. When Faith appeared, the maid got up and left.

'Ah, *domina*. Good morning. I worried about you all the night long, my dear. I've already ordered breakfast.'

And who said the little old dear was senile? Faith asked herself as she pulled up a chair. Her breakfast plate was there almost before she sat down. Eggs and country ham, toast, coffee, and papaya juice. 'I didn't realize it, but I'm starving,' Faith said.

Lady Sunny, who was feasting on a stick of dry toast and a cup of coffee, made a face. 'I think the last real meal I had was almost twenty-five years ago,' milady said. 'Dicky was so stern about dieting, although he never did himself. Unfortunately the women of my family have the tendency to run to——'

'Excess weight?'

'Fat,' milady said firmly. 'Now, tell me about your adventure.'

And Faith did. Milady gave her the utmost attention, leaning forward with both eyes glued on her *domina*. And it wasn't until Faith had covered every aspect of the situation that milady signaled for another pot of coffee and sat back in her chair.

'It's too bad that lives were lost. That's always the problem with terrorist activities, I understand. This is the first occurrence on St Kitts in all the years I've been here. You must take some time off to rest, my dear, and I shall call your mother and tell her the entire tale.'

'You mustn't do that, milady. It would be a waste of your time.'

'Not so, young lady. The highest degree of management takes place when the seniors show concern for their workers. There are those who let material things get in the way, but personal relationships take first place in the true management cycle.' And she stopped to sip more of her coffee. 'And it is never a waste of time.'

Why is it, Faith asked herself, that I'm getting a lecture on management? Did I really screw things up last night?

'You didn't tell me how well our workers did at the fire,' milady continued.

'I—our workers?'

'Oh, my dear, you must have been so busy. Yes, our workers. Sixteen of our men are organized into two volunteer pump crews. They responded on the second alarm. You should make a point of dropping in on them today. Our fire house is just behind the stables.'

'I—will, of course.'

Milady made a half-hearted motion toward pushing her chair back. Instantly two maids were there to help. 'Of course,' the old lady commented as she managed her first step or two, 'our *domina* might well have stayed here to organize and control our own people. *N'est-ce pas*?' And with that she walked away, leaving Faith to finish her meal.

Faith crumpled her napkin and tossed it into the middle of the plate. 'And that, Faith Latimore,' she told herself in a soft whisper, 'is where you get the rest of your management instructions!'

'Does the *domina* require anything further?' Mary was at her elbow.

'The *domina* requires instruction on how to manage her job,' she said, sighing. 'Would you believe, in all the instruction I took at university, not once did I get any information on how to run a volunteer fire department?'

'I'm sure that missy will learn in a hurry,' Mary returned. 'We have a book.'

'I'll bet we do,' Faith replied. 'Now, I intend to spend the rest of the day with my computer terminal and the office mail.'

'Ah, the computer—and the mail? I will arrange it.'

'What's to arrange?'

'Nothing important, *domina*. In the past it has been the custom to bring the computer machine to your sitting-room for only two days a month. It will not take long to re-install, if you wish.'

'Ah, that's why I didn't see it until yesterday. Well, have someone bring it up. *Domina* wishes,' Faith said very firmly as she pushed her chair back and headed down the ramp at flank speed.

Faith knew that there was a huge intercom system in the house, but had no idea where the terminals were located. But she was not really surprised when she got back to her sitting-room and found the machine sitting on her table, chuckling at her. A moment later one of the maids whom she hadn't met came in with a basket full of mail.

'*Domina* asked for the mail?'

'I did. And you are——?'

'Julia, ma'am. I work in the business department.'

'Thank you, Julia. That's all I need for now.' The girl, whose face was as solemn as a statue, offered the merest curtsy and left, silent as a mouse.

'Well, I didn't set *her* on fire.'

'Julia?' Mary was behind her, having come in as silently as Julia had left. 'Yes, Julia has many troubles.'

Faith shrugged and settled down to the mail. There were bundles of it, divided already into sections marked "Bills" and "Receipts" and "Correspondence". And finally, the thickest of all the packets—one marked "Personal". Faith put that one aside; she had no instructions about reading Lady Sunny's personal mail.

'Mary, do we have a messenger of some kind? I seem to have accumulated all of milady's personal mail.'

Her maid hesitated for a moment. 'Yes, Miss Faith. There are messengers. I will take the mail out to them. You wish that they go directly to milady?'

'I guess I do,' Faith said, noticing the hesitation. 'Don't I?'

Mary took a deep breath. 'If *domina* wishes the mail to go to milady, it shall surely go there.' She held out both hands to receive the packet, and then swished out of the room at full speed.

'Well, what do you make of that?' Faith asked herself as she spread out the business mail and prepared to decipher it. By noon she was down to the Receivables, and her spreadsheet was as full as her stomach was empty. Her lunch appeared without instruction—a tasty ham sandwich, a pot of tea, two cookies and an orange. She nibbled as she continued her work.

By three that afternoon she had worked her way through all the mail, and was running through some of the computer programs. And her head was getting heavy, and her eyes began to blink.

'*Domina*?' A gentle hand was at her shoulder. She opened one eye and saw Mary, with a platoon of men and women behind her, all waiting patiently for—what? 'If *domina* has finished,' Mary said hesitantly, 'Thomas is here to talk to you.'

Faith turned and looked at a young man she'd never seen before. He appeared more than a little bit frightened, and for the life of her Faith could not reason why. 'Yes,' Faith said, 'what can I do for you, Thomas?'

'*Domina*,' Thomas almost stuttered, 'is it that my entire department is discharged from our job?'

'Not that I know of,' Faith said, still confused. 'Why do you think you might have been?'

'I went to milady, but she had no answer. She said you were in charge of everything except her.'

'Yes, I believe that's so. So why would you think you have been fired?'

'Because, ma'am, you picked up all the mail and then sorted it. And then I see you have done all the work to handle the material,' Thomas said. 'And that's my job. Julia is the mail clerk. Clairmont is the accountant. Lucy and Primrose assist him as bookkeepers. And every day we handle the mail and balance the books and answer the business letters—unless you have fired us?'

'Julia is the mail clerk?' Faith asked, suddenly knowing why he was so upset. 'Oh, lord, what have I done?' she said, suddenly aware that she'd disturbed the order of the household day. 'I'm sorry,' she said, 'I didn't mean to take your jobs. No, you're not fired. I came in early this morning and saw the mail on the table so I just grabbed it all and got to work on the bills. Please excuse me; I didn't realize that would upset anyone.' Faith paused and saw a look of understanding pass over Thomas's face.

'Listen,' she continued, 'I promise that I will never pick up the mail again. Only someone must tell me what I do with all this.'

'*Domina*, if you will excuse me, when we finish with the checks, the messenger will bring them to you for signing. When we finish with the letters we will bring them to you for your approval—and signature. And when everything else is done, we will come to you for tomorrow's instructions—ma'am.'

'And Lady Sunny?'

'Lady Sunny never looks at anything, ma'am. She says keeping track of business gives her wrinkles. And when you meet with her for dinner she will say, "Everything is all right, *domina*?" and you will say, "Yes, milady."'

Faith looked around the circle of smiling faces. 'Even if everything is *not* all right?'

'Even so,' Mary said. 'Lady Sunny knows everything that goes on in the house and in the business, but if someone brings something to her attention she feels she is bound to *do* something about it, and that she does not want. So, do *not* bring anything to her attention. *Domina* does everything.'

'Well, I never had it put to me like that in law school or business school.' Faith got up and stretched. She had been tied to that chair for hours. 'And you, Thomas. You report everything to me?'

The young man grinned at her. 'If there is anything to report,' he agreed.

'Then I would like all this mess removed, and done correctly,' Faith said, sighing. She wandered slowly into her bedroom. 'I'm going to take a nap, Mary. You wanted something else, Thomas?'

'The administrative department is sure that this has all been done correctly, ma'am. But we will go over it and enter it into the books just for practice.'

'Thank you, Thomas, but don't be so sure of that. What I did is all on the computer. You'd better check it with an eagle eye.'

'Thank you, *domina*.' Thomas beamed at her. 'I'll try to get it sorted out. We very seldom get the day's business on the computer until midnight. That work is done by the computer-machine department.'

'Thank you, Thomas,' Faith said as he left the suite. 'I'm going to have a headache, Mary. I am definitely going to have a terrible headache!'

'Missy,' Mary asked, 'aren't you going to eat lunch? That's why you have the headache.'

'Mary, I had lunch at noontime.'

'Lunch? That was only a snack, *domina*. Now is teatime, and you need something substantial. Dinner, you know, is not until nine o'clock. You need something now.'

'All right,' Faith said resignedly. Mary, moving as gracefully as always, left the room. 'Now where was I?' Faith asked the walls. 'Oh, yes. How many people does milady have working for her?' Her computer blinked at her. She walked back to the desk and formulated the question. The machine rattled and grumbled and beeped. 'Fifty-two,' the machine spat out, and then ruminated like an old cow. 'Fifty-three. One hospitalized.'

'Oh, shut up, wise guy,' Faith snorted. 'You're the smart type of machine that made me decide I didn't want to be an engineer.'

Mary came in at that moment with her tea-tray. '*Domina* was talking to someone?'

'Myself,' Faith confessed. 'The dumbest girl I know.'

'*Domina* makes the joke.' Mary grinned at her and set the tea-tray before her. 'Lady Sunny tells us all about you before you come. Now, you eat?'

The cook had made a pasta salad with fresh tomatoes, olives, onions and ham chunks all covered in a spicy oil dressing.

'This is a plot between you and the cook, isn't it?' Faith asked Mary. 'You figure that if the meal looks this good I'll stop and eat slowly while seated at a table.' She looked at Mary with a smile and continued, 'Well, even if it isn't a plot, I will eat it at the table by the window.'

'Plot?' Mary repeated innocently. 'Cook and me, we don't plot nothing. But we'll be glad if you eat at leisure instead of gulping it down without enjoying it. Besides, Cook wants to know if you like this dish. She's trying it out on you first, before serving it to milady.'

'Oh,' Faith said, 'that's comforting to know.'

She was aware that, once again, the workers at Rose Cottage were showing her how devoted they all were to milady. She, Faith, might have an important job, but Lady Sunny was the center point of the household.

She put these thoughts aside and sat at the little table that looked out over the back of the estate, and the gardens that milady loved to putter in at all hours. It reminded her of her mother, Mary Kate, and the garden she so carefully tended. The air was heavy with scents. It was almost overpowering.

But the cook didn't want critiques on flowers. She wanted—— The salad was delicious and she would recommend it for milady's table. It was just tangy enough that she could feel her tastebuds awaken, and the chopped vegetables in with the pasta were just crunchy enough that she could feel them in her mouth. But then again, she'd always liked crunchy food, even crunchy peanut butter. Which was, when you got to thinking about it, an oxymoron—sort of like military intelligence.

'Mary,' Faith said to the hovering maid when she'd finished eating, 'give my compliments to the cook and tell her that I recommend this for milady's lunch some-time. Did you have any?'

'Yes,' Mary said, 'I tried it. The cook would not allow me to serve you something that the staff hasn't tried.'

'You don't sound enthusiastic about it,' Faith said, looking closely at her.

'It wasn't like anything I've ever had before,' Mary said, 'but it wasn't all bad.'

'I wouldn't tell Cook that,' Faith laughed as she got up from the table and let Mary clear the dishes. A Byzantine system, Faith told herself. There are food-tasters, and food-tasters for the food-tasters, and—and so on until we get up to Lady Sunny!

'No, *domina*,' Mary said, also laughing. 'I don't ever criticize the cook. You never know what she's going to make next time.'

Faith sat back at the computer screen and then, re-membering her promise to Thomas, shut it down. She had a crick in her neck. She stood up to get the stiffness out of her body.

'Missy,' Mary said as she came in the suite door, 'are you finished for now?'

'Yes,' Faith said. Then, suddenly hit by a bout of curiosity, she asked Mary, 'How is it that you're always so at hand when I need you?'

'What do you mean?' Mary asked.

'What I'm trying to ask, and doing a fairly bad job of it, is how did you manage to come in just at the moment I'd finished working at the computer?'

'Oh,' Mary said, relieved. 'I've been looking in every couple of minutes since lunch to see if you were done so I could help you get ready for the evening.'

'Mary,' Faith said, 'what else do you do, besides look after me?'

'I help with the house chores and I help in the kitchen sometimes. But now that you're here, you are my primary job,' Mary said with some pride.

'Did you take care of the last *domina*,' Faith asked as she walked into the bedroom with Mary following.

'No,' Mary said. 'Domina Pearl had Justine to help her. When she was married, Justine went with her, which was only proper. When you came it was my turn to be the *domina*'s maid.'

'Oh,' Faith said, just a little astounded. She'd never had someone to do so much for her, and so cheerfully. 'I'm going to take a shower,' she told Mary. 'Please pick out something for me to wear this evening.' She had the feeling that the last request was strictly unnecessary as she could hear the closet doors being opened before she even left the bedroom.

The hot water gradually eased her aches. Faith leaned back against the heated tile walls and relaxed.

CHAPTER SIX

FAITH came down the ramp, dressed in Mary's choice—
a pale green silk tunic top with matching green silk
palazzo pants. Her long, light brown hair was French-
braided very neatly. There was some security in knowing
that she looked calm, clean and up to Mary's standards.
Mary, she was coming to understand, had the same tough
standards as Mother Latimore did.

Lady Sunny, who was escorting Police Inspector
Wheeler, met her on the ground floor. 'Oh, good,'
milady said as she saw Faith standing at the foot of the
ramp. 'Come and join us.'

Faith followed dutifully, and when they reached the
veranda she saw that Harry was already there. He was
newly-showered and dressed in a black shirt and trousers.
All he needed was a silver string tie and a black som-
brero to be a typical Texas cowpoke. Bad guys always
wear black hats, she reminded herself. Good guys wear
white hats. And he's already wearing black cowboy
boots.

He stood as milady and the inspector came outside.
There was a crooked little grin on his face, as if he was
reading Faith's mind. But that's impossible, she told
herself, when I don't know my own mind! She gave
herself a good shake to restore her equilibrium.

'The inspector has come to talk to you about the incident yesterday afternoon,' Lady Sunny said. 'But first,
Inspector, would you care for something warm or cold
to drink?' Milady was gracious, as always. It was bred
in her bones.

'Something cold, if you please, milady,' the inspector responded, 'and non-alcoholic. I'm still on duty.' It was plain to see that Inspector Wheeler was another of milady's admirers. He fairly beamed as he accepted her offer. Napoleon appeared out of nowhere with the inspector's drink. The glass sported a sprig of mint. A moment later two of the maids appeared, bearing refreshment for the rest of them.

'Now,' Wheeler said, after he'd taken a healthy swig of the iced tea, 'we do have some questions for you, Mr Holson.'

'Yes?' Harry responded. He moved to one side and Lady Sunny settled into his vacated chair. The lady looked tired.

'How much damage would you say was done?'

'Not as much as expected,' Harry said, consulting a little card he took from his shirt pocket. 'The blast reached the steelwork on only the first two floors. The wood framing above that burned out. Our best estimate is that it did three hundred thousand dollars' worth of damage. Our insurance will cover most of that, including medical costs of the injured men.'

'And, as a construction man, what does that suggest to you?'

'Inexperience,' Harry replied. 'They didn't know what they were doing. In fact, if they had set the bomb twenty feet farther south, the most they would have done was scorch the paint on the outside of the tower.'

'Hmm,' the inspector said. 'Not very experienced? That would tend to rule out revolutionaries. We keep a close tab on the three or four who think they are underground here on the island. We had some small amount of trouble several years ago, during the time that Anguilla broke away from St Kitts and Nevis, but we managed to scotch the troublemakers of that little affair in a hurry.'

'Besides,' Lady Sunny interjected, 'why would a revolutionary group want to burn down a hotel? It wouldn't have any place to meet!'

'Just so,' the inspector murmured almost under his breath.

Harry gave him a suspicious look.

'So that brings us to the second possibility,' the policeman continued. 'Somebody or some group that has a grudge against your company.'

'Of course, there's always the environmentalists,' Harry mused. 'Although we've answered most of their complaints with our new building techniques. We did have an ecological survey, done by DeWolf and Harmon, which proved that everything was going well. Still, there's a hard-core group that objects just because we're changing things. You know them? They want St Kitts to remain permanently the way it was fifty years ago, even though the hotel could help the islands become self-sufficient.'

'Yes, we know them,' Inspector Wheeler said. 'But they suffer a terrible deficiency. They're growing old. I can't think of a one of them who could execute this bombing, even done poorly.'

They looked at each other for a moment, sipping their drinks. And then Lady Sunny broke the silence. 'Drugs,' she said.

Faith looked at the little old lady, startled. For the past two or three days she had developed a strange feeling about the earl's daughter. The "sunshine" was all on the outside. Inside, milady seemed to have more than a few of the answers about what was going on in Rose Cottage and on the island.

'Drugs,' the inspector pondered. 'Well, it's true that drugs are invading the island, and that Frigate Bay has been the ideal spot for landing them. And now you've closed them off by your construction project, I don't really know what effect that has had. I'll check with our narcotics squad later today. You all must know that the future is catching up to St Kitts as well as the rest of the Caribbean. The drug culture is moving north out of South America. Drugs? Hmm.' He pulled out his notebook and scribbled to himself.

'Now, Mr Holson, it may be a little far-fetched, but do you have any personal enemies on the island?'

'Not that I'm aware of,' Harry answered. 'Not anyone who would resort to this sort of action.'

'The reason I asked,' Inspector Wheeler said, 'is that not all our citizens are happy singers of songs and fiesta celebrants. Jealousy and revenge are behind most of the petty crimes we deal with from day to day; it's entirely possible that they could be behind this bombing.' He stopped and tapped his pen on the table in front of him. 'How about jealousy? Can you think of anyone, inside or outside your company, who might be jealous of you or your company? Jealous enough to try and destroy you and your hotel?'

'I can't imagine anyone that jealous of me,' Harry answered with a small smile. 'I don't mean there aren't arguments of various sizes within the company, and cliques who would like to argue from foundation to roof, but most the people involved are old construction hands. Now, if one of *them* had decided to blow up the hotel, it would have been blown halfway to Nevis, that's for sure!'

The inspector nodded. 'And, of course, this explosion showed none of that kind of experience. So now how about the other possibility? Is there anyone on the island who would want to take revenge on you personally for some real or fancied insult?'

Harry paused for a moment. 'No, I don't think so,' he said finally. 'But you know,' he said, 'if things had been going normally I would have been right at that site myself. Instead I was out, on Lady Sunny's orders, enjoying a picnic at Brimstone Fort.'

'Lucky you,' milady commented. 'Sometimes it does good for young people to listen to orders from their elders.'

'I'm only listing the possibilities,' Wheeler reminded Harry. At Harry's nod of agreement, the inspector continued. 'I'm intrigued by the thought of smugglers. Frigate Bay has long been the ideal site for smugglers. By putting up a hotel where you are, you might have angered them.'

'What would they be smuggling?' Faith asked as Harry and the inspector thought over this last possibility.

'I'm still thinking of drugs, *domina*,' the inspector said. 'There are other things—American cigarettes, for example—but——'

'So, you're suggesting,' Harry interrupted, 'that the smugglers may believe that we're ruining their business. Do you think this explosion might have been a warning? Or an attempt to stop construction totally?'

'I'm not sure which one it was supposed to be, if either,' Wheeler said. 'But I do know that you've been making some enemies among that lot, not only with your construction but also your anti-drug campaign.'

'Well,' Harry said, 'I'll admit that if our anti-drug campaign works it means they'll be out some customers. Is there a Mafia element here?'

There was another quiet moment. And then Lady Sunny dropped another statement into the pool of silence. 'As you know, I sit on the governor's council. I understand that the island is undergoing some serious problems. The gamblers from Cuba a few years ago, and now the South Americans, looking for bases closer to the Colonies.'

The inspector covered his mouth and coughed, embarrassed. 'The—er—United States, milady. Yes, that's possibly true.'

'I'd say, then, that drug-smuggling would be a very logical reason for the bombing,' Harry said. 'Particularly since our security guards have chased some suspicious people away from the site late at night.'

'Yes,' Inspector Wheeler said, 'we know about those incidents.'

'Do you mean to say,' Faith wanted to know, 'that smugglers were trying to use your hotel site as an exchange point?'

'We believe so, *domina*,' the inspector said. 'We're keeping our eyes and ears open on this subject and we've increased our surveillance. All we really know is that they are here. We have some scraps of evidence as to who they are.' He sat quietly for a moment, and then scribbled something more in his notebook. 'But you have provided us with one of the miscreants, *domina*. We will certainly question her most thoroughly.'

'Haven't you spoken to her?' Harry asked.

'Only for a moment,' the inspector said. 'Just long enough to discover her name, and the fact that she lives at Friends' Estate. And then her lawyer showed up. I doubt we will get anything further from her. But rest assured we shall ask questions. Mind you, everything we've discussed is strictly theory, and strictly confidential. Not until we get more facts can we make a judgement.' He flipped his notebook closed and rose, stretching.

'It's getting late, my dear inspector,' Lady Sunny said. 'Won't you and Harry stay for dinner? We'd love to have your company.'

'Thank you, milady, I'd be honored,' Inspector Wheeler said. 'But I am not dressed.'

'I'm sure we must have something that you could wear,' milady said. 'But you must know that I find a man in uniform to be well-dressed for any occasion.'

'Milady,' Inspector Wheeler said, laughing, 'I am truly honored and I will be indebted if I might have the temporary use of one room with a telephone so that I may complete some duties for the day.'

'Of course.' Milady was gracious, as always. 'Napoleon, please show the inspector to a room which he may use for his business. He will be joining us for dinner.'

'Yes, milady.' The butler led the inspector off to the requested room.

'Well, my dears,' milady said fondly, scanning the young couple still with her. She leaned over and patted Faith's hand. 'Harry, has your father left the island?'

'Yes, milady. He had to return to Puerto Rico to arrange some new financing. I hope that I meet the dress requirements for dinner myself?'

'Oh,' milady giggled, 'I would love to have dinner with a real cowboy. Dicky would have envied you. He so wanted to be a cowboy when we were younger. But he found that cowboy boots gave him blisters. And then he found he was allergic to horses. It was such a pity. He would have been a wonderful cowboy. We bought a ranch in Mexico and were planning to stay there, but then the allergies—— Well, you know. So, we sold the ranch and moved here. Oh, well, we found happiness here. I do wish that Dicky hadn't been taken from me so early in our life together.'

'You have stood your tragedy well,' Harry said. He took her hand and bowed over it while he kissed her fingers.

Oh, lord, Faith thought. He's been studying up on European customs. I wish—— She blushed and ducked her head. I wish it were me he was kissing? But all he offered her was a quick smile and a nod. Faith Latimore revised her thoughts. I wish I were wearing cowboy boots, she told herself. I'd kick him right on his anklebone a time or two! Damn the man!

Lady Sunny, misinterpreting Faith's frown, smiled her happy little smile. 'Don't worry about me, *domina*. I'm just tired. A certain lack of sleep. I'll be fine once I'm dressed for dinner.' She got up and started toward the door to the house. And then said, over her shoulder, 'The two of you should go for a walk in the garden. The flowers are all in bloom. It's marvelous down there.'

Both Faith and Harry had risen to their feet when milady got up. They turned to each other and watched the little black-dressed figure disappear into the house. 'Well,' Harry said, 'I don't know about you, but that sounded like a royal command if ever I heard one. Will you join me for a walk in the garden before dinner?' He took her hand and bowed over it, turning it palm up.

She could feel the touch of his tongue on her hand. When she had been a hell-raising teenager back in Massachusetts, a kiss on the palm had meant a great deal more than an ordinary buss. And this was one of the most erotic sensations she had ever experienced. She made an effort to put her heart back in place. 'Of course,' she said, when her heart had stopped pounding. 'I'd love to see the garden.' And then she turned her back on him, trying desperately to suppress the spreading blush.

He held out his hand to her and when she offered her own he led her across the veranda to the ramp leading to the gardens and the grounds in back of the house.

'This has been one hell of a day, hasn't it?' he asked.

'But there have been rewards,' Faith answered as they entered the formal English garden. Paths of crushed white seashells wandered gently up the slope of the hill.

Not too far away a white paddock fence closed off the pastures from the gardens. 'Rewards . . .' she murmured.

'What rewards?' Harry wanted to know.

'We saw the dawn break this morning,' Faith said, and Harry nodded, 'and it looks as if we'll see the sun set tonight.' He nodded again. They continued to walk. One of his hands closed on hers.

Startled, she jerked free. Truce, she told herself, not a full-scale peace treaty. There are still too many unsolved questions.

'I never realised how beautiful the beginning and end of a day could be. And there's Isabelle, enjoying her retirement,' she said.

'With your morning attitude,' Harry said with a smile, 'who'd dare to wake you for dawn?'

'No one,' Faith said, half smiling in response. 'Not if they value their lives.' She was feeling so confused. She wanted nothing to upset the fragile calm.

'Do you know the names of these flowers?' Harry asked, as if he was making casual conversation.

'I know some of them,' Faith admitted, 'but only a few. My mother and my sister Hope are the gardeners in the family.' But then she noticed that milady's gardeners had put small signs in front of each of the bushes.

'Look,' she said with a laugh in her voice, 'milady has very thoughtfully provided us with labels.' She bent down to read the sign in front of the bush before them. 'These are called Dicky's Darlings. I've never heard of that sort of rose before.'

'Well,' Harry said, 'the way Dicky adored Lady Sunny, doesn't it make sense that she would get a variety of her favorite flower named for her?'

'After everything else Dicky has done for her?' Faith said with a fond smile. 'No, I don't think that's so strange.' She started to walk away from the bush toward the fence that separated the garden from the paddock.

Harry stood up from where he was bending to read the rose's name and followed her to the pasture fence. She turned to face him, leaning her back against the fence posts. Isabelle came trotting up to join them. The old mare butted her head into Faith's back, pushing her forward. Faith looked as if she was going to fall over. Harry held out his arms—and she fell into them. The horse whinnied.

'There seems to be a conspiracy in this house toward matchmaking,' Faith said, just a little breathlessly.

'If that means that you end up in my arms,' Harry said, 'then I'm all for it.' He gently brought her closer. 'You have the most beautiful eyes in the world and I'm going to kiss you.'

He wasn't looking at my eyes at all, Faith told herself, but what the hey?

If he was asking permission to kiss her, he certainly didn't plan to wait for a response. Besides, Faith told herself as she relaxed in his arms, what would I say? No?

Not a chance! He is a find and a half. He's just what I want for Christmas, Easter and the anniversary of the invention of the cotton gin. All those major holidays. If only there weren't so many doubts in her mind. At this point his arms tightened around her, a heat-flash danced up her back, and all rational thought left her mind.

The kiss was spectacular. Faith felt as if she was viewing the Fourth of July fireworks and the New Year's displays on the Esplanade in Boston all wrapped up together. Spectacular. She had been kissed before, by some very good practitioners. But this one left them all behind.

The kiss could have gone on forever, but eventually Harry lifted his head. 'If we don't stop this soon we'll be late for dinner.' His voice had a rasp in it. A sort of strain.

'Late for dinner,' Faith muttered. 'Oh, no—no, we can't be late for dinner.' Her mind settled; she shuddered. Too close for comfort, Faith Latimore, she told herself.

On the other side of the fence Isabelle whinnied. 'It's a great night for females,' Faith murmured. The mare leaned across the barrier and nuzzled them both, leaving her clean wild scent as a marker on Faith's fingers.

'But,' Harry said, 'first things first. I have to thank Isabelle.'

'Thank Isabelle?' Faith was more than a little confused. 'Isabelle? The horse? Whatever for?'

'For just being herself,' Harry said as he went over and scratched the animal's head. He fed her the piece of sugar he had put in his pocket earlier, just in case. But Isabelle had done her duty without any incentive. She nuzzled Faith again, and once more the girl ended up in his arms. Harry gave up his interest in hurrying to the table. He had other appetites in mind.

Some minutes later, holding hands, they walked up to the veranda. Milady was sitting out of their line of sight. She stood as they came up, and smiled happily at them. Faith was struck with a sudden thought. Lady Sunny was in no way as sheltered and naïve as she appeared.

Or was she? Look at the way she had stage-managed the walk in the garden. She had probably instructed Isabelle to come over and push her into Harry's arms! No, that wasn't possible, was it—talking to a horse? She wouldn't put it past milady to have some witch tendencies. Voodoo was popular in all the Caribbean islands. But to talk to a horse? No, that would be silly. Lady Sunny was just what she appeared to be. What am I thinking of? Faith asked herself frantically. I'm letting my imagination get the better of me!

'Hello, my dears,' Lady Sunny said. 'How did you enjoy the garden?'

'It's lovely, milady,' Harry said. 'And we got to see Isabelle. She seems to be in good health.'

'That's nice, my dears,' Lady Sunny said. 'Let's go inside. I believe the inspector is ready to join us.'

Faith and Harry followed milady into the house to the drawing-room, an intimate lounge where the bar held sway. He was still holding her hand, and no amount of discreet wrestling was going to set her free. The inspector was already there with drink in hand. It was probably a gin and tonic; that seemed to be the sort of drink a policeman would have in his hand, Faith thought. He still wore his uniform, although Faith could see that it had been pressed and freshened.

'Good evening, milady,' the inspector said as he stood at Lady Sunny's entrance.

'Good evening, Inspector.' Lady Sunny offered her hand as he came over and bowed.

'I'm honored to be here this evening with such delightful company.'

'You have always been a flatterer, Phineas,' milady said, taking her due as the lady of the manor. Before she could turn, Francis, the barman, had her usual drink ready and waiting for her at the small table next to her special chair.

'Thank you,' milady said quietly. Faith was beginning to believe that one of the reasons milady was so well-liked was her sense of courtesy.

'*Domina*?'

'A glass of tonic water with a slice of lemon,' she ordered.

'Beer,' Harry ordered, without waiting to be asked.

'A real cowboy drink?' Faith murmured.

'Yes, ma'am,' he drawled after taking a large gulp from the mug. 'All us real cowboys drink beer. Have you ever heard any true country-western songs about a man drinking wine? I'm pretty sure the cowboy union has grounds to throw you out with no recommendation if you're caught with anything but a beer. Besides, it's hard to balance in a saddle if you're holding a martini glass.'

'Yes,' Faith said. Her hand was finally free. She tucked it behind her back. 'I can just see John Wayne bellying up to the bar in one of his movies and asking for the house wine.'

'It kind of loses its punch when they ask, "what's your poison?" and the answer is, "Chablis,"' Harry said.

They were interrupted before they could continue. Lady Sunny said, 'Come over here, you two. The inspector will get bored with only me for conversation. We could use some cheerful topics.'

'Yes, milady,' Faith said. She jumped nervously in front of Harry, avoiding his searching hand, and led him over to join the other two in the conversation circle.

They chatted for about twenty minutes and then the double doors of the dining-room opened, and the butler announced, 'Dinner is served.'

The inspector led milady to her chair at head of the table and Harry steered Faith to her chair. When he had seated Faith, Harry took the seat beside her and held her hand beneath the level of the table. What in the world am I doing? she asked herself. Our brief separation was supposed to have restored me to normality. Normality? What have I been doing for the past hour? Walking in the garden? Kissing him? She tugged at her hand, just when the meal was served. He gave her a reluctant release. She pulled out her kerchief and wiped her palm. Get a grip on yourself, girl, she thought. He *still* may be Jack the Ripper!

The meal was served quickly. Roast beef and Yorkshire pudding, with a salad of tropical fruits and a side-dish of vegetables. 'A favorite meal,' milady said. 'I was talking to the Queen Mother about it just last week. We went to school together, you know. Her father was an earl as well.' She sighed. 'Those were exciting times.'

'The Queen Mother?' Harry took a quick swallow of beer to wash down a slice of beef. 'Do you mean as in the Queen of England?'

'Yes,' milady said calmly. 'The Queen Mother and I are cousins, thrice removed, but she recognizes the connection. She and I went to school together in our youth. Before she married into the Royal family.' She said this very calmly. Her dinner companions sat and stared at her in amazement.

It seemed to Faith that Harry and Inspector Wheeler were inclined to disbelieve. She, on the other hand, believed every word of it. Why not? The daughter of an earl? If milady said it was so, it was so. 'What did you talk about with her?' Faith wanted to know.

'We normally talk about just anything that comes to mind. The fire at the castle, the little family problems. Nothing important. It's my birthday in three weeks, you know. She always manages to squeeze in a call around this time of year.'

'That was rather politic of her,' Harry said. 'Particularly when her family's life is being spilled over all the tabloids in the world.'

'In my younger days,' Lady Sunny said, at her haughtiest, 'the Press knew its place and stayed there. They did not meddle or print scandal of their betters. It breaks my heart, the way the world has deteriorated.'

None of the three with her at the table wanted to touch her last statement, so a small pool of silence grew while they finished off the food on their plates.

While the plates were being cleared, milady looked at Faith and said, 'O'Malley and Mary came to me this afternoon to ask my permission to marry. It isn't really necessary, but the asking has become a custom here at Rose Cottage. Arrangements will have to be made.'

'Yes, milady,' Faith said. 'Do you have any suggestions, or have they voiced any preferences to you on the subject?'

'I'm led to understand that they would like a large ceremony,' milady said.

Faith noticed that milady grew animated at the thought of a wedding. 'I'll have to give it some thought,' Faith said. 'And I'll have to talk to Mary and O'Malley about their wants and desires.'

'That sounds lovely, dear,' milady said. 'You take care of it.' She had done her part. The rest was up to the *domina*. Which brought up her next thought. 'You know, my dear,' Lady Sunny said, 'I so enjoyed riding in Dicky's new automobile that I believe we should have two more. One for Sundays and another for emergencies.'

'Yes, milady.' Her voice might be calm but internally Faith was appalled. Milady's attention had been distracted by Inspector Wheeler, so Harry leaned over to her.

'Something wrong?' he whispered.

'She wants two more automobiles. Do you know how much a light blue limousine with diamanté bumpers costs?'

'With what?' Harry nearly choked on his after-dinner coffee.

'Diamanté bumpers! I looked at the bill this afternoon. The additions we make to the vehicle are *very* expensive.'

'So how much is she spending?' Harry asked, without really thinking about the question.

'It's not any more than she can afford, it just causes my Yankee upbringing to crawl in a corner and hide.' She wasn't about to tell him that the total of one car, including bodywork and the painting, was seventy-five thousand American dollars.

'It must be a hefty sum,' Harry said, 'if it upsets you to spend Lady Sunny's money, of which, you assure me, there is an abundance.'

'She is *not* running on empty,' Faith said firmly. 'It's just that the idea of spending this much money at one time makes me want to cry. Milady tends to be rather nonchalant about spending her money. Of which there *is* an abundance.' Her hand was trapped again. She pulled, trying to get it back, but Harry wouldn't let it go. Instead, he brought it to his mouth and kissed her palm. When she tried to pull away he grinned.

'I don't know what overcame me, *domina*. Let's not get angry at each other. We've been getting along so well.' She tugged at her hand again, but not for love nor money would he let go!

Faith turned her eyes to the rest of the table. Milady was watching them with a satisfied look on her face. 'Faith, I believe that one of the new autos should be plain black for Sundays, so that we may go to church in the proper style.'

'Yes, ma'am. With all these new vehicles we should train some more drivers to help O'Malley. Perhaps we can have O'Malley train three new men.'

'See to it, *domina*,' Lady Sunny said offhandedly. 'That is why you are here, is it not? We shall retire so that the gentlemen can enjoy their port.'

Once again, Lady Sunny had put Faith in her place and reminded the *domina* of her position and responsibilities. But Faith was not going to let that get her down. She bent over and kissed Harry's cheek while rising from the table. It startled him so much that he released her hand. Which she had intended.

'You seem to be getting along well with Harry,' milady said as they sat themselves down in their respective chairs.

'For the moment, yes,' Faith said as she watched Lady Sunny pull out her embroidery.

'Only for the moment?' Milady darted a quick glance up at Faith. 'Oh, well. I had a lovely long talk with your mother yesterday. She's quite a remarkable woman, isn't she?'

'My mother? I—er—— Yes, she is,' Faith answered with a great deal of pride and love in her voice. As she reflected on her mother, she was hit by another thought having nothing to do with her parent. 'What do you think of a shipboard wedding?'

'For you, my dear?' Lady Sunny looked up intently at her. 'Have you and Harry got that far already? How lovely! Yes, I can see you marrying on board the *S S Bellerophon*. And if you don't suffer from *mal de mer* you and Harry could take her out for a honeymoon cruise.' The old lady chuckled at that.

There's something fishy behind that, Faith told herself. I wonder what?

Faith knew she had to interrupt Lady Sunny's train of thought or she would have Faith married to Harry in a flash. 'No, milady.' She interrupted Milady's chatter. 'I don't mean me, I mean Mary and O'Malley. We could have the service and the reception all on board the *S S*— er—what did you call it?'

'*Bellerophon*, dear,' Lady Sunny said with a sad little smile. 'The name was Dicky's choice. He so wanted to be a man of the sea.'

'But he suffered from seasickness?' Faith continued. It would seem rather appropriate. Dicky had suffered from almost everything that prevented him from being the man of his dreams. Or were they milady's dreams? There was a point there that nagged her. Had Dicky really been the ruler of the roost?

'Unfortunately yes,' milady said. 'We saw the ship and fell in love with it. Dicky felt that a ship should have a name to live up to, a name filled with a proud history.'

'I'm sorry, milady,' Faith was forced to admit, 'but I don't know the history of that name.'

'Don't they teach history any more in schools?' Lady Sunny was shocked. 'Possibly it was omitted in your youth because you went to school in the Colonies...'

'Possibly,' Faith said as apologetically as possible. 'But——'

'My dear,' Lady Sunny said with pride, 'the *HMS Bellerophon* was one of the flagships of the British fleet during the Napoleonic wars. It was the scourge of the French.'

'Oh,' Faith said, taken aback. 'British history was rather skimpily done in my school. I'll have to read up on the subject.'

'But you went to a school in England,' Lady Sunny protested.

'Yes, but I was in graduate school and we didn't read history.'

There was a pause in the conversation. Milady's needles flashed in and out at high speed. 'Are you happy, my dear?' Lady Sunny asked out of the clear blue sky.

'Yes,' Faith answered quickly, and then thought about her answer. 'Yes, I am *very* happy.'

'I'm so glad that you and young Mr Holson are getting along so well now. I knew that given time the two of you would hit it off splendidly. As you have. It makes me feel very proud.'

Faith gulped. 'I'm delighted that you are happy, milady,' she said, just a little wary about milady's words.

'That is, if I remember correctly, what I was hired to do for you.'

Milady smiled happily and went back to her embroidery. Faith took up a magazine she had started to read and then put it down again. She wasn't going to be able to comprehend what she read while she was in this mood. And what was this mood? She was totally confused. She was wary. Marriage was not her favorite topic. Lady Sunny peeked up at Faith and smiled. From the adjacent dining-room they could hear the men laughing.

James, the footman, came into the sitting-room with a small silver tray. On the tray was a fax sheet. James put the tray in front of Faith. She apologized to Lady Sunny and picked up the paper. And read it twice. After the second reading her anger began to rise. She tore at the corners of the paper as her rage grew. Harry, that rotten Texas cowpoke, had lied to her!

'Is something wrong?' Lady Sunny asked.

'Nothing that I can't handle, milady,' Faith said shortly. Preferably with a hammer and some *very* long nails on the body of one Harry Holson. At that moment, Harry and the inspector came into the room. Faith knew that milady would suggest a hand or two of bridge. She liked to play when she had a foursome. Probably Dicky would have liked to be a gambler, but he was allergic to playing-cards? Stop that, Faith, she told herself. That was uncalled for. Dicky was probably a wonderful man. He certainly was perfect for milady. Just calm down now, woman. You'll be able to pound on Mr Harry Holson when the time is right.

'Would you care for some bridge, inspector?' Milady asked hopefully.

'I would be honored, milady,' Inspector Wheeler answered, 'particularly if I may partner you. You are one of the best players I have ever known.'

'Thank you,' milady said. 'Why don't we play over there?' She pointed to the card-table already set up on the other side of the room. 'And we can play against these youngsters.'

'What a wonderful idea,' Harry said. He turned to Faith and asked, 'How good a bridge player are you?' He noticed the fierce expression on Faith's face. 'What's the matter? I thought we had worked everything out before dinner. Truce?'

'Truce, hell,' Faith muttered. 'What happened is this.' She held out the fax for Harry to read. The message was from her brother, Michael, who was chief executive officer of Latimore Construction now that their father had decided to take things easy.

'I sent a query to my brother Michael about the loan to your company. This is what he sent back.' She passed the paper over to him. The message read, 'RE YOUR REQUEST INFO ON LOAN HARRY OR NATHAN HOLSON. HANOR.'

'If you don't understand cable-talk,' Faith hissed with scorn, 'that last part "HANOR"—means "have no record". You lied to me, Harry Holson. And the proof is right here! I'll play cards as your partner, but if I had a knife I'd rather cut your throat, you damn liar!'

He stared at the flimsy piece of paper. 'Must be some misunderstanding,' he muttered.

'Yeah, misunderstanding,' Faith returned. 'Play your cards. I'll get to you later.'

CHAPTER SEVEN

'THAT'S the last trick,' Lady Sunny said after playing her final card, 'and it's late. I must be off to sleep soon. Beauty rest is very important for a lady of my years.' James, who had been standing behind her most of the evening, pulled back her chair.

'Thank you, milady,' Inspector Wheeler said. 'It's been a long time since I played with such an excellent partner.'

'Can I offer you two gentlemen a ride to your destinations?'

'No, thank you,' the inspector said. 'I've got a police car assigned to me and I must make one more official stop before I'm off to home and bed.'

'I'd certainly appreciate a ride back to the site,' Harry interjected.

'Are you intending to stay the night on the site?' the inspector wanted to know.

'Yes,' Harry responded. 'I don't think I can ask any of my men to stay where I wouldn't. If something is going to happen tonight, I want to be Johnny on the spot.'

'Be careful,' the policeman said gravely. 'We had enough destruction today.'

'Of course,' Harry reassured him. Although he gave the assurance rather offhandedly, Faith was pretty sure that if anyone showed up at the work site tonight, planning some mischief, the police would be notified—later.

'*Domina,*' Lady Sunny said over her shoulder as she left the room, 'please escort the gentlemen to their cars.'

'Yes, ma'am,' Faith acknowledged. She certainly wasn't thrilled about the prospect but milady had been fairly specific. On the other hand, it offered one more opportunity of pricking the conscience of Harry Holson.

She turned to the two men. 'This way, gentlemen.' She waved her arm toward the door to the hallway.

Harry grabbed her arm and tucked it under his. He towed her along as he walked to the front ramp where the cars were waiting. 'Goodnight, Inspector,' Harry said cheerfully. 'Say goodnight, Gracie.' He gave an extra tug on her arm.

'Goodnight, Inspector,' Faith said with as much charm and cheer as she could manage at the moment. But not even the long evening and the enforced card partnership dampened her anger.

'Say goodnight, Gracie,' Harry repeated. 'That's a line out of an old radio show.'

'I'm not that old,' she said, doing her best to freeze him out with words.

'You don't remember George and Gracie?'

'I don't remember radio!'

A moment of silence. 'This is all one big misunderstanding,' Harry said as he kept a death-grip on her arm. 'I'll get to the bottom of the whole confusion and get back to you. I'll straighten it all out, Faith. We'll be laughing about it by tomorrow. You'll see.'

'I don't think so.' Faith tugged mightily, trying to get her arm free. 'I don't like liars or bullies. And you fall into both categories, Mr Holson. The only thing I'll be laughing about is when you're revealed to the world as a deceitful person. Then I'll be laughing, believe me.' She stopped to catch her breath. 'Now, Mr Holson, your ride is here. Please go. And don't be in any hurry to come back, if you please. And don't leave your fingerprints all over the car.' With that last bit of sarcasm, made in what she hoped were cutting tones, she tried to turn and go back up the ramp.

But Harry still had a death-grip on her arm. When she turned, she turned into him. 'Not so fast there, missy,' Harry said with anger in his voice. 'I'm not a liar. And if you want to see a bully, here's a real one.' He pulled her into his arms and brought his lips down to her protesting mouth. Faith struggled, but was unable to break free from his grip. Gradually it was no longer a competition, strength against strength. Like heady wine she savored him for just a second too long, and was lost. Her head began to spin and there were sounds of bells in her ears. She made one last spurt to break away, and finally gave up. She went limp in his arms, and then, instead of fighting him, she was cooperating in her own seduction.

Faith hadn't an independent thought in her head. Response was all she knew. Where his penetrating tongue led, she followed. The kiss lasted forever and not long enough. Her response to Harry was unthinking and nearly primal. His tongue demanded an answer. She provided it. His lips stroked hers and he took her bottom lip between his teeth. Then he was kissing her again, full on the lips. His mouth moved, stealing little kisses over her face and on her earlobes. It was magic—until the moment when he pulled away from her and set her a little apart. She groaned, and scrambled back to him, trying to re-ignite the flame. He pushed her away. She heard him, as if from a distance.

'Damn,' he muttered, and pushed her away again. But she couldn't stand on her own two feet. She grabbed for his shoulders. He offered two hands to help, but only for a second.

'Don't be a bigger fool than you have to be,' he said softly. 'You love me and I love you. Don't try to build walls between us, *domina*.'

The words cut into her illusion. She regained her sense of balance, and moved away from him. Her boiling anger took fire again. She wiped her lips disdainfully with the back of her hand. 'You didn't mean all that, Mr Holson?' she mocked.

He growled something indistinguishable, and gave her a little shake. She was even angrier. 'I'm not in love with you. I couldn't love a man like you,' she gritted from between clenched teeth. She pulled back and slapped him as hard as she could. Harry grabbed her hand as she tried to slap him again. Faith managed to get her hand free and turned quickly to run up the ramp. It was difficult to run; her tears were flowing magnificently, blinding her.

She blundered into the house. Napoleon, the butler, looked as if he might try to stop her, but then just opened the door and stood out of the way. Faith kept running. She slammed into her suite and set her back to the door. Sanity and logic, she told herself. I can find it all here. All the things missing from my relationship with Harry Holson. In here are all the records and information I need to do my job. I don't need any man around to mess me up. Even if it is the man of my dreams. Come on, Faith, admit it to yourself. He's right. You do love him. But you can't trust him!

Sleep was going to be a hard-won prize tonight. Faith's brain and imagination were running at top speed. Admitting to herself the truth of her feelings was a major enlightenment. She looked out the window of her suite and saw that there was a full moon. Things clarified in her mind, thoughts tumbled after each other. One pursued her—how about jumping off the top of Brimstone Hill?

The moon cast a pearly gleam across the grounds. Slipping out of her dinner outfit, she put on a pair of jeans and an old sweatshirt, clothes she had brought from home. Comforting clothes, clothes she would never wear in front of milady—or That Man!

Faith was, by nature, a self-assured personality, but after the problems with Harry she needed to renew her identity. Where had she put Faith Latimore? She sneaked out of the suite, down the ramp to the veranda. It felt silly, practically tiptoeing out of the house, but she didn't want an audience. Somewhere out in that bright moonlight her real persona, Faith Helene Latimore, attorney-at-law and *domina* of Rose Cottage, was hiding, and she must find herself.

She went down to the garden and over to the fence bordering the pasture. Isabelle had evidently gone to the barn to get her night's sleep because the pasture was empty. Faith leaned on the fence and stared at the Caribbean Sea. With the moonlight coloring the water and the steady lullaby of the surf, she fell into a trance. Against her will her brain started to relive the few happy moments with Harry. Faith remembered reading a book once in which the heroine had said, 'Scoundrels are so easy to fall in love with but they can so easily break your heart.' When she'd read that statement she'd been contemptuous of women who could fall in love with men like—like Harry Holson. Now she remembered and could identify. But, she thought, no matter how much I may be attracted to him, he is *not* getting a cent from Lady Sunny's estate. I'll fight him tooth and nail over *that*. I can get over him. I'll wake up tomorrow and get to work. I'll erase him from my life. Who ever heard of someone dying from a broken heart?

She turned from the vista and went back into the house, walking as softly as when she had left. Upstairs, she took a shower and put on her cotton pajama shorties, and then went to bed. She slept almost instantly, but about three hours later she woke from a nightmare. Someone was screaming.

A soft hand touched her shoulder gently. '*Domina*?'

Faith squirmed, and managed to open one eye. She was sitting up, with the sheets wound around her legs like a pair of convict chains. 'What?'

'*Domina* was screaming.'

'Yes. I——'

'Rose, *domina*. I am part of the nightwatch. Can I——?'

'Nothing,' Faith interrupted. 'Nothing. I was dreaming.' She watched as the maid efficiently unwound her from her sheets, smoothed her pillow, and helped her to lie down. 'Thank you—Rose.'

Rose adjusted the sheets over her, then quietly withdrew. Faith tried to relax. The dream? Faded now, escaped into the night. Something about Harry standing on the tower of his hotel, and a man pushing him from behind. Pushing him off the tower. Faith shuddered. It was foolish to try to get back to sleep with that dream hovering over——

Rose, standing in the shadows at the door, watched with a smile on her face. She came over to the bed and briefly checked, then went back to the living-room of the suite and pushed the little communications button that connected every part of Rose Cottage to the security office. 'Three o'clock,' she reported. '*Domina* is wake up with a night-horse.'

'Nightmare,' the guard corrected.

'Yes. Nightmare. Now she have gone back to sleep.'

Dawn. A quiet, tropical dawn. The sun was still below the horizon, hiding in the depths of the Atlantic Ocean. A thin green line of light painted the pre-dawn darkness and was gone. A moment of silence. The herring gulls

came awake and launched themselves on their first noisy
ocean sweep. Close in, the island birds came awake with
their own chatter, and began combing the beaches for
their breakfast. A particularly persistent rock dove
perched on the Rose Cottage veranda outside Faith's
bedroom and seemed about to burst with its own song.
Faith stirred.

'Noisy creature,' she muttered.

'He sings of love, *domina*.' Mary, already bustling
around the room, picking up the mess that Faith had
left the night before.

'Bah! Humbug!' Faith tried to shut it all out by
burying her head in her pillow. To no avail. Today, she
reminded herself, is the day when I really take control
of Rose Cottage! She threw her pillow on the floor and
staggered out of bed.

'Bah, humbug?' Mary inquired. Faith was fully awake
by now. She dashed for the shower. A little cold water
would finish her requirements.

'Yes,' she told her maid as she passed her by. 'There's
no such thing as love. Bah! Humbug!' She stepped into
the shower and almost screamed in agony at the cold.

'*Domina* will learn better,' Mary said placidly. 'The
green dress?'

Faith burst from the shower cubicle, her teeth chat-
tering, and was instantly enveloped in the big bath-towel
that Mary held ready.

'*Domina* will learn better, what?' she asked as she did
a wardance on the floor. 'Cold water?'

'Love,' Mary said.

'*Domina* knows more about love than she has a need.
Just because you're getting married it doesn't mean that
every woman should. Rub the middle of my back. Ah,
just there. Now—the green dress?'

And so, dressed, nightmare banished and heart restored, Faith went out to the veranda for breakfast. And almost screamed again.

Lady Sunny was there at table, her usually placid face alive with interest. And, sitting opposite her, Harry Holson.

'Isn't this lovely?' milady said. 'Dear Harry has time to design our garage and swimming-pool! Aren't we lucky?'

'Lovely?' Faith groaned. 'Lucky?'

'In a manner of speaking,' he responded. 'The explosion didn't do a great deal of damage, but it was just enough to require some further architectural work by our company people before we can resume building. So we have a sort of holiday.'

'And some months ago dear Nathan promised me a swimming-pool,' milady said. 'Isn't that convenient?'

'And garage?'

'I added that this morning,' Lady Sunny said. 'Everything just seemed to fall in place, *domina*. I'll be in conference most of the day with our manager from Bangladesh. But luckily I have you here, dear child, and you can stick close to Mr Holson and supervise things.'

'How lucky I am,' Faith groaned under her breath as the lady got up in that half-trot she normally used, and disappeared into the house.

' "Everything just seemed to fall in place",' Faith mimicked. 'Do you have a voodoo doctor on your staff?'

He grinned at her. 'White magic only, *domina*.'

'Damn,' she muttered, and reached for the breakfast juice. Which was empty. 'Damn,' she repeated.

He stood up and stretched. 'C'mon, girl. Let's get down to the pool area.'

'In case you didn't notice,' Faith snapped, 'I haven't had breakfast yet. And I'm not going to go an inch without eating!'

'Materialism,' he said. 'There's a higher value than eating.'

'Yeah. I notice you said that after you'd filled your belly!'

'Belly? I thought ladies referred to it as a stomach?'

'Ladies don't refer to it at all if they can help it,' she snapped.

Her coffee had arrived. She sipped at it desperately, as if it were a blood transfusion. Two lonely pieces of toast came next. Faith restrained herself. Her initial urge was to stuff both pieces in her mouth at the same time. Harry Holson was leaning over her—casting a shadow?

She glanced up at him. 'Getting an eyeful, are you?'

He grinned. 'So to speak.'

She glared at him and buttoned the two top buttons of her dress. 'Voyeur,' she snapped.

He shrugged. 'I'd probably be insulted if I knew what that meant,' he said. 'But what the devil? It's a nice view, and you've got a lovely pair of——'

'All right, I'm ready,' she exploded, pushing her chair back into his stomach and standing up. 'Damn man,' she growled. 'If I were two feet taller you'd be more careful with your sexual abuse!'

'Sexual abuse?'

'You're damn right. Standing over me, looking down my dress, saying I've got a lovely pair of——'

'Earrings,' he interrupted. 'There's something sexual about earrings? If there is, you shouldn't wear them.'

'I could easily hate you,' she snapped. 'More than I do already, I mean.' She was up on her feet by now. He took one of her small hands and towed her down the veranda toward the back, and she tagged along as best she could until they went around the curve that took them out of sight of the front of the house.

She dug in both feet and they skidded to a halt. 'If we were back Stateside,' she panted, 'I'd have you put away in the slammer for this harassment. Or, better still, I'd have my brother Michael rearrange your face for you!'

'Oh? Your brother is the family enforcer?'

'My *little* brother——' She slowed down to emphasize all the words. 'My *little* brother is six feet seven, he weighs three hundred pounds, and he played left tackle for the Notre Dame football team!'

'Well...' He drawled it out, Texas style. 'I'm impressed. In fact, I'm downright scared. When he gets here I'll be in a lot of trouble?'

'A lot!'

'In which case, I might as well have my fun now.' He pushed her gently against the reinforced concrete and put his hands on the wall on either side of her head. She tried a wiggle or two, but was unable to escape.

'I'm not afraid of you,' she boasted, and then, just a dab more timidly, 'What are you going to do?'

'Sexual harassment,' he said, 'is all in the eye of the beholder. And if you're not afraid of me, you ought to be!'

The world seemed to go into slow motion. His head came down, a millimeter at a time, until his lips touched hers, and then instantly withdrew.

'Huh!' she said, mustering up all her available bravado. 'I've been kissed better than that!'

'Fool girl,' he muttered. 'Worse than that!' His head came back down again, this time lingering, sealing her off from the world around her. She could feel his tongue probing at her mouth, and thought to say something about that, but the release of her lips allowed him entry. At the same time one of his hands slid down her neck and shoulder, under the flap of her bodice, and ended up resting casually on her breast.

'No,' she managed to get out. A very timid 'no'. A 'no' that hardly anybody could possibly believe, be-

cause her hands ran up the front of his shirt and wrapped
themselves around the nape of his neck at the same time.

'No?'

'I——' His hand refused to be still. It stroked and
teased the peak of her breast and came to rest on her
expanding nipple. Faith Latimore had played this sort
of game a time or two before, but suddenly it became
not a game, but a war. Male summoned female to the
age-old combat. Fire greater than the tropical heat
smashed up into her brain; her automatic nerve system
screamed for relief. She pressed closer to him, so close
that only two thin pieces of cotton separated them, and
not very well at that. She squirmed.

And Napoleon the butler, coming up behind them,
said, '*Domina*, I brought your breakfast.'

Faith, startled, went into shock. First, because
someone had witnessed her response to Harry, and
second, because she had responded so thoroughly. Harry,
on the other hand, just leaned back with a big smile on
his face. He was relaxed; she was shaken. Another black
mark against you, Harry Holson, Faith thought. 'Thank
you, Napoleon,' she finally managed to stutter.

Behind Napoleon one of the big footmen was carrying a large silver tray. There was a plate-sized silver
cover over the center of the plate, a Thermos of coffee
and a big glass of papaya juice, freshly squeezed, on the
side. Faith smiled graciously and quickly turned away
from them all so that she could rearrange her blouse.

'It is my pleasure, *domina*,' Napoleon said as he passed
her and led them down off the ramp toward the large
banyan tree, in whose shade two of the maids were setting
up a table and two chairs. Behind the house, but higher,
it offered a fine view of the property, the island, and the
sea. Faith hadn't noticed the table before.

Napoleon gestured, the footman lowered the tray
gently, and all except the butler disappeared.

Flustered, Faith asked, 'Has this table always been here?'

'No, *domina*,' came the answer as he assisted her to sit and then uncovered the food on the plate. 'But wherever *domina* wishes to breakfast there will be a table.' He bowed and took himself off.

'Well, saved by the bell,' Harry said, chortling.

'Oh, shut up,' Faith snapped.

'Shut up? The lady's manners are falling to pieces.'

'Any minute now the lady is going to cloud up and rain all over you!' A pause to draw breath. 'Why don't you show me where the swimming-pool is to be put?'

'I can't do that,' he protested. 'Leave a lady all alone with her breakfast? There's enough for two. I believe I'll join you.'

'Oh, yes,' Faith growled. 'Do make yourself at home.' She filled both coffee-cups and glared at him, as if challenging him to pick one up.

He did.

'Did it ever cross your mind that perhaps I don't want company for breakfast? Especially *your* company?'

'Never crossed my mind, because you love me, darlin'.' Harry smiled, a large, rather fatuous grin.

At least that was what she told herself. It was a large, complacent, foolish and inane expression. She ducked her head and addressed herself to the Belgian waffles topped with strawberries and whipped cream. Harry joined her. She watched him out of the corner of her eye. Convincing myself I'm not in love with him is going to be an uphill struggle, she told herself. He doesn't seem to remember that the rules have changed. Come on, *domina*. You can disabuse him of this stupid notion. Love? Hah! All you need to do is to remember his lies. He's after milady's money. Don't forget that. You can keep your cool just as long as he stops kissing you every time you turn around!

'If you don't chew faster,' Harry said, 'the way you're continuously stuffing your mouth, you'll choke. Are you having a race? Is the food going to run away?'

'I was just thinking,' Faith managed to say, after dropping her fork and taking a large swallow of juice.

'About what?'

'About you and this fly-by-night construction company of yours.'

'Ah, there!' He leaned across the table. 'You *are* interested in me! Admit it!'

'Stop it,' she commanded, 'before I throw up. Yes, I'm interested in you. I'm trying to figure out how I can have you arrested for malfeasance.'

'I didn't learn about that while I was in school,' he said. 'Malfeasance.'

'That's the word. Hire a lawyer to explain it to you. Are you planning to eat *all* the waffles?'

'I had to hurry,' he responded. 'You were eating like a——'

'Don't you dare!'

'Like a starving child.' That genial smile again. Lord, he was an attractive man, Faith told herself. Fight back!

She settled back in her chair and laid down her eating tools. She was appalled at herself. She never ate this way! Mary Kate Latimore had drilled proper etiquette into her and all her siblings. One took small bites and chewed thoroughly. Pausing between bites. One didn't try to stuff an entire Belgian waffle in one's mouth without swallowing between bites. Even if your fork was going automatically to your mouth without any thought on your part. One especially did not make rude suggestions to the man who—to any man!

'You'll notice that I've decided to be polite to you,' she said calmly.

'I can see that,' Harry said. 'The question is, why? But——' he smiled and held his hands up '—who am I to try and stop you?'

Faith sat and chewed while looking at him. 'Where do you intend to place this swimming-pool?'

'Right there.' He gestured in front of him.

'That's solid rock!'

'A slight misstatement. That's rock, but it's not solid. Old volcanic rock never is.'

'And you'll what? Dynamite it? If you do the whole cottage will slide off the side of the hill.'

'So you did learn a little something, growing up in the Latimore family. Of course we won't blast it. Jackhammers and muscles, Miss Faith. You'll be swimming in it within thirty days. Tiles and all.'

It was all possible, she told herself, except how in the world was he going to get those heavy compressors up that hard-scrabble hillside to do the work?

He might have just been reading her mind. She heard the hum of engines overhead. He pointed toward the seacoast. Two massive helicopters were parading up the side of the hill, each lifting machinery in its net. Faith gritted her teeth. Helicopters—compressors—manpower. He *would* build here, whether she wanted or no! Her face flaming, she stood up and shook her finger in his face.

'You'll not make yourself twenty-million dollars on this two-bit swimming-pool,' she raged.

He smiled at her lazily. 'No,' he agreed. 'Just a little bit at a time, *domina*.'

'And I'll make you account for every cent,' she threatened. 'Every nickel. Every dollar! See if I don't!'

'Oh, I believe you will,' he said agreeably. 'Don't forget the garage. We'll make a bundle on the garage.'

'Ooh.' She stamped her foot. 'You are the most disagreeable man I've ever known!'

Napoleon appeared at her side again. '*Domina* is not pleased with the breakfast?'

'*Domina* would have preferred roast Texas beef,' Harry offered.

Faith gathered up her tattered moralities and stomped back up the ramp, heading for the center of the house.

By four that afternoon Faith had completed her inspection of all the departments in Rose Cottage and was exhausted. 'I don't understand,' she told Robert, the head of the business department. 'I can't find a thing that's wrong. Not a thing.'

'*Domina* is too kind,' Robert replied. 'But then we are but two months past our last yearly inspection.'

'Yearly inspection?'

'The auditors come from London and look at everything, and then the lawyers, and then Lady Sunny comes. Once every year.'

'Lady Sunny inspects? She knows——'

'Every employee, every department, every contractor. Milady knows everything. *Domina* is going to tea?'

'*Domina* might as well,' Faith said, sighing. Another illusion all shot to heck. Lady Sunny might be the flighty bird she appeared to be, but once a year she waved her magic wand and turned into the chief inspector from the Inland Revenue!

Faith folded up her notebook and made for the late afternoon sunshine on the veranda. One thing she knew for sure about Rose Cottage. One never had to go looking for something; one merely had to appear on the veranda and, presto, the thing she wanted would come to her.

And this time it worked to perfection. No sooner had she sat down by the most convenient table than Napoleon appeared, leading a train of maids. 'Tea, *domina*?'

There was only one hitch. She nodded, the team sprang into action, but before she could settle back That Man was beside her, sliding into the chair opposite. 'Thought I was going to be late,' he said as he rolled down his sleeves. 'I'm still a growing boy, and us Texans need our nourishment.'

'Growing boy?' She snorted her disbelief.

'We can't all come in nice packages, the way you do,' he said.

Think, Faith commanded herself. Have I just been complimented? Or is this another back-handed insult? There was no way to tell. She shrugged in despair and opened her mouth to say something, only to be put on hold again as Napoleon maneuvered his team to the tea service. Tea and crumpets, cucumber sandwiches, small frosted cakes—everything that one read about at the Ritz, but which was seldom available except in the Old Country. Faith took a very satisfying sip of the Earl Grey, and sighed contentedly.

'I still want to see the plans for the garage,' she said as she raced him for the best cake.

'And so you shall,' he told her. 'I've had my people out looking for you all day. Do we eat, or do we go and look?'

'You could just tell me,' she told him. 'Especially, you could tell me what the costs are. And the timetable. I don't suppose you have the swimming-pool finished?'

'Give me a break, lady. We just started today. And we had to stop at two o'clock so as not to disturb Lady Sunny's nap.'

'Of course,' she murmured, having given milady's comfort small shrift herself. She watched him munch on the last cucumber sandwich. Without thinking she said, 'You must take a lot of feeding up, Mr Holson.'

'That's true,' he agreed. 'But I'll never make it on cucumber sandwiches. Ham sandwiches, that's what I need. Or maybe even steak sandwiches—things like that.

You should take notes, you know. You'll have to be able to handle these things afterward.'

'Afterward?' And immediately clapped her hand over her mouth.

'After our wedding,' he said.

'You should live so long! And that's a very strange-looking tea you're drinking.'

He tilted up his cup and drained it. 'Do you say so?' he inquired.

'Beer?' she asked. 'They brought you beer!'

He set his cup down and grinned at her. 'They'll bring you anything you want in Rose Cottage,' he said. 'Well, almost anything. Now, about the garage. It will be built out behind the present building, to have ready access to the roadways. Our plan allows space for six automobiles, not including the vintage Cadillac.'

'Lady Sunny will never stand for throwing out Dicky's famous first car! Never!'

'And never we will,' he said, chuckling. 'We'll refurbish the old garage completely, and leave the old car——'

'May I join you?'

They both looked up. Chief Inspector Wheeler was with them again.

'Have a chair, Inspector,' Faith insisted. 'You look tired.'

'I am that,' he admitted. 'Crime is rampant on St Kitts and Nevis today.' He lowered himself into a chair. The maid in attendance whipped out another cup, and Faith poured.

'Rampant?' she teased him.

He took a massive sip of tea, ignoring the heat of the liquid. 'Rampant,' he repeated, his eyes twinkling. 'Two robberies, three assaults with intent, and one car thief.'

'Good lord. Have some pastries. And what brings you to Rose Cottage this afternoon, Inspector?'

'I think perhaps we may have narrowed down the case involving the explosion at Mr Holson's construction site,' he said.

They both sat up, interested. Harry was unable to restrain himself. 'Well?'

'Well, there's been some—complication. The young lady at the hospital. The one you both pulled out of the wreckage. She wasn't as badly injured as we had first thought. A lawyer appeared for her this noontime, bailed her out, and whisked her off someplace or another. Naturally, we have closed all exits to the island.' One more sip emptied his cup. Faith refilled it, her fingers jittery with excitement.

'And that's it?' Harry asked.

'Not exactly. Lovely cakes. I like that mint flavor.'

'I'll be sure to tell the cook,' Faith said sarcastically. 'Now, about——'

'Yes,' the policeman interrupted. 'We discovered that the woman is the girlfriend of one Vincent Declaur, over at the Friendly Estate. You remember him?'

'Oh, the young man who raced us,' Faith said. 'Him?'

'The bad-tempered young man who raced you, and whom Mr Holson here aggravated by making a citizen's arrest.' One more sip of tea, and an expansive sigh. 'Our Mr Declaur has gone to ground. Disappeared. Our Mr Declaur has some small knowledge of explosives. Our Mr Declaur is noted among the young set for his violent temper. And our Mr Declaur has dropped out of circulation. But there aren't many ways to get off the island, you know. We'll round them both up sooner or later. In the meantime you both had better watch your backs. It's lucky you're both located at Rose Cottage. I've assigned some men to keep an eye on things.'

'You mean I have to stay here at the cottage?' Harry asked. His voice was mournful, but there was triumph sparking out of his eyes.

'I don't believe in waiting until I'm pushed,' Faith said. 'Won't you stay the night with us, Mr Holson?'

'I do believe I will,' he said, grinning. 'And after dinner we can look at the garage site. How does that sound?'

Faith didn't want to tell him how that sounded. And besides, Lady Sunny was coming out on to the veranda to join the crowd, and *she* would certainly not be prepared for the kind of language that would be required.

CHAPTER EIGHT

THE hand fell lightly on Faith Latimore's bare shoulder. 'Go away,' she muttered, and rolled over. The persistent hand fell on the other shoulder. 'Keep your hands off me!' It had been a terrible night, filled with wild dreams. Most of them starring the evil Harry Holson. In the last one he had been doing things to her that she never could have imagined possible. Things that brought on a great deal of sinful pleasure. 'Go away! Keep your hands to yourself!'

'*Domina*?'

She opened one eye. Daylight flooded her room. The tropical air hung heavily, humid enough to be called rain if one were not too particular. 'Oh, Mary. I'm sorry.' She swung her feet to the floor and threw the blankets off. Her head wobbled.

'Miss Faith has had a bad night?'

'Very bad. You couldn't imagine how bad.'

'*That Man*?' Mary said emphatically.

A groan. Her head felt a little loose on her shoulders. 'Yes, That Man.'

'Here is coffee, *domina*. Open both eyes. It restores the vital juices.'

Faith attempted to follow the instructions. 'It also burns the fingers,' she added grumpily.

'Miss Faith has drunk too much of the alcohol last night?'

'Not a single drink to drunk,' Faith responded. 'Drink to drink.' A sigh of disgust. 'Alcohol to drink. English is a terrible language. I'm going to skin that man alive!'

'Drink the coffee,' Mary urged. 'The opportunity awaits you.'

Both of Faith's eyes came open. 'Now what have I done?'

'Nothing yet.' Mary's musical voice was sympathetic. 'But Lady Sunny awaits you at the breakfast-table. That Man is with her.'

'And?'

'And milady says she can never agree to a decision about the garage until *domina* says.'

'Oh, God!'

'Yes. *Domina* does not go to church regularly. Perhaps you should go and ask Him.' A rustle of sheets. 'More coffee, *domina*. I think you require very much coffee in the morning. Three cups, perhaps.'

'Pour.' Faith's voice cracked and her fingers shook the cup. How is it possible, she asked herself, to awaken totally angry? How could a man insult me so badly, even in my dreams?

'He is really a nice man,' Mary commented as she sorted through clothing for the day. 'Not as nice as my man—but when one gets older one has fewer choices, no?'

Which caused the whole room to explode. Faith was ejected, fully clothed, not quite sure what had happened. Older indeed! Fewer choices—well! And when she arrived at table Lady Sunny had gone, and only Harry was there. You have to admit, she whispered to herself, that he's a fine broth of a man, but I hate him none the less.

'Well, it's about time,' he commented as one of the maids held a chair for her.

'For what?'

'For—dammit, Faith, why do you always trip me up with these stupid questions about questions?'

'Because they're not stupid,' Faith returned. 'I was busy.'

'Doing what?'

'I have a collection of Agatha Christie mysteries, and I'm going over them trying to lay out a perfect murder plot.'

'Murder is treated very harshly on the island,' he said.

'Not if it's justified. Where did milady go?'

'She said something about using the new car to go to luncheon with the Governor.'

'Ah.'

Napoleon rushed up, trailed by a fleet of maids.

'*Domina*, I beg pardon. I thought——'

'No problem. May I have my usual breakfast?'

'Of course.' He clapped his hands and his troops scattered to their stations. Faith sighed with contentment as she sipped her fourth coffee of the day. And then, more placid than before, 'And did you explain what the inspector said? And what did Lady Sunny think about it?'

'You and milady have a lot in common,' he said. 'She said, "So it wasn't smugglers or gang warfare. Just a little frog so proud that he wanted a larger swamp to croak in."'

'Yes, but even little frogs can cause problems. Did you bring the drawings and estimates for the garage?'

He handed her a single piece of paper. She set her coffee-cup down to peruse it. 'Forty-two thousand dollars? American dollars, I suppose?'

'You're so right.'

'Ah, you really meant it that you planned to make a bundle on the garage?'

'You can't blame a boy for trying,' he said as he passed over an envelope of additional drawings.

'And we get all this for that price?'

'Every bit of it. And in any color you desire. But I didn't include any diamanté stapled into the walls. What's the trouble?'

'Nothing. I'm reading the drawings.'

'Don't tell me now that you're a lawyer who can read blueprints.'

'Okay, I won't tell you. But that's *my* croissant, Mr Holson.'

She read and munched. He sat and looked. This girl is too smart for me, he told himself. I could get married up with her and wind up with my head in a basket! But will you look at her? There's no doubt in my mind that I've got to have her. Lord knows, she might even teach me something. But bossy! Whoever would——?

'That looks all right,' she interrupted as she passed the folder back to him. 'Only with six stalls for parking those big limousines you need to put in a wider axial turn area. Maybe as much as three feet more.'

'Well, I'll be——' He flipped through the pages of blueprints and studied the one to which she referred. 'Maybe,' he commented. 'Come and see.'

'I don't need to see. That's what blueprints are for. Run along, like a good fellow. Mary and I have to start on the planning for her wedding. Unless you're a specialist in weddings, as well?'

He rattled his chair back from the table, rolled up his blueprints, and grumbled off. Faith watched him stride off down the ramp. Massive strides, she told herself. I'm Jack and he's the Giant? Massive shoulders. Furrowed, angry face. Serves him right. So now we have two of us grouches on duty at Rose Cottage! My mother would give me holy hell. That's not the way to get a man to work for you!

'*Domina*?'

Faith, startled, dropped her coffee-cup. O'Malley, the big chauffeur, was at her elbow. And behind him Mary—

giggling. A wrong thought, she told herself. For some reason O'Malley looked even bigger than usual, and she knew by now that he was not the largest male on the staff. 'Napoleon tells me that milady says you wish for to inspect the ship,' he said.

'I do. We do. Mary and I. Is it convenient?'

'Last time someone wants to inspect t'ship was Easter four years ago,' he reflected. 'For the orphans from the mission, you understand. They scarred the ship up somethin' awful.'

'So it's not convenient?'

A reflective silence from the boatman.

Mary's giggle ran away with her. She nudged O'Malley in the ribs with one of her sharp elbows. 'For the *domina*,' she reminded him.

'For the *domina*, of course.' His face changed; the clouds disappeared and a smile consumed him. 'It is always convenient, *domina*.'

'Well, then, let us go down to the sea,' Faith announced with great majesty, which she then killed by giggling. 'And inspect ships.'

Out of the shade on the veranda into the bright, warm sunshine of a tropical morning, the trio came down the hill to the *S S Bellerophon*. The ship sat at the docking pier with the presence of an aged queen. She was bigger than Faith remembered. Bigger and grimly gray, like a true ship of war.

'She's lovely,' Faith mentioned before she got to the next sentence. 'Why isn't the gangplank down? We're going to need it lowered for the party. And for milady. And, by the way, how do *we* get on board?'

'Yes,' Mary said seriously, 'I'm not going to ask milady or my grandma to climb up the ropes like you do, O'Malley.'

'The gangplank we have raised,' he said. 'To protect the ship. There are them as would come aboard and steal things, Miss Faith. Would you believe?'

'Steal?' Faith was startled. Thieves in St Kitts? In Boston, perhaps, but not here!

'Yes, Miss Faith.' O'Malley was quick to defend his ship and his honor. 'Before we put up the gangplank people got on board and took some instruments of the navigation. And they even carved initials on Master Dicky's favorite banisters in the lounge.' Faith could see that this desecration of the banisters—of Master Dicky's banisters—was far more important than stealing navigation instruments. 'I've tried for long time to sand down the spots to get rid of these desecrations, but it doesn't work, *domina*. They scarred my ship for life!'

'*My* ship,' Faith told herself. Possessive care. I wonder if all the servants think the same way? O'Malley was about to add a dozen or so pages of complaints. Before things got out of hand, Faith interjected, 'How do we get the gangplank down?'

'Need electricity for that, Miss Faith. Once we're on board I'll show you the generator that I wipe.'

'I'd rather you show us the way up,' Faith said with some trepidation.

He went to the side of the ship and reached for a rope that dangled from the deck rail about twenty feet above their heads. He shinnied up the rope with the ease of a monkey. 'Just take hold of the rope, *domina*, and climb up. Like so.'

'Oh, yeah,' Faith muttered as she went over to the rope. She looked at it and knew instantly that she wasn't going to be able to go up that way. She'd always hated the rope climb in gym class and she wasn't going to like it now. She stepped back and looked up at the trusting face of O'Malley. 'I can't climb that rope. I'm in a dress.

Is there some other way up, please?' And I don't have the guts for it anyway! she added silently.

'We have a cargo net,' O'Malley announced after a moment's thought. 'I could put that over the side and then you could climb up the net like a ladder. Would that do?'

Faith looked at Mary; Mary looked at Faith and nodded slightly. 'All right, do that.' While he went to toss the cargo net over to them Faith said, 'We have got to get up there to look at the generator so we can get the gangplank down. I have the funny feeling that I should have inspected the ship *before* I mentioned it for the wedding.'

Mary's face fell. '*Domina*, don't worry. O'Malley and me, we like the idea of the ship for our wedding. We know you'll take care of everything.'

'Yeah, here we go again,' Faith muttered. *Domina* knows everything. *Domina does* everything. Where did I leave my witch's broom?

'Here it comes,' O'Malley shouted from the ship's deck above their heads. The women scattered. He threw the net over the side. It landed with a massive thump on the dock before them.

'And the net isn't in any too good a shape, either,' Faith told Mary.

The smile on Mary's face faded just a bit. 'I'll go first, *domina*,' she was quick to say.

'Be my guest,' Faith answered, 'but be careful. That net doesn't look all that sturdy.'

'I be all right, *domina*,' Mary assured her. 'I don't weigh too much.' At which she took hold of the net and very carefully and slowly climbed upward. Faith noticed that she went widely around one area in particular.

'Be careful around here, *domina*,' Mary shouted down to her. 'A lot of the rope is frayed badly.' Faith screened her eyes and watched as the cargo net swayed. Her stomach felt just the least bit queasy, and she hadn't lifted a foot off the dock as yet. But far overhead Mary reached out a hand to her muscular fiancé, who hauled her up and over the rail.

Mary stood back to catch her breath. Faith, still on the dock, watched as the maid gave the boatman a lecture, including much finger-waving under his nose. A wavering wind flushed the last words downward. '—and I'll tear you to little pieces, boatman. *Domina* is——' And the wind faded.

'Any time you're ready, Miss Faith.' Mary leaned over the rail and yelled down the dockside.

Why is everybody so cheerful? Faith asked herself. You're up there all safe and sound and I'm the one that has to make the climb. Oh, all right, I know that you just made it and did it safely, but do I have to? She took a quick look around. A round dozen of the staff from various parts of the cottage were watching her, all with big expectant smiles on their faces. Yes, I have to, or I'll never be able to give orders here again, she told herself. She gritted her teeth and started her climb. It wasn't like climbing a ladder but then again it wasn't shinnying up a rope either. The lattice of ropes shifted at each movement, and her light shoes slipped off at every opportunity. Which left her dangling and spinning, with the sky twisting away from her, and her stomach in a near state of rebellion. She was unable to force herself to take another step.

Halfway up the side of the ship she froze in place, afraid to go down, and unable to go up. The net suddenly took on a life of its own, dancing and swaying as if someone were running up from below her. Faith closed her eyes, commanded her hands to remain glued to the cross-stitches, and tried desperately to recall at least one of the prayers she had learned at church. 'Make it stop, God,' she muttered.

And the deep voice beside her said, 'Why not?'

She opened one eye, knowing the answer already. Harry Holson, next to her, balanced as carelessly as a spider in its web, grinning.

'Why are you trying to kill me?' she wailed. The sky shifted again, twisting crazily, and his big arm came around her shoulders.

'Steady, lady,' he said, almost in her ear. 'Don't freeze up. We'll go up together, me right in back of you. Right?'

'I'm scared of heights,' she told him. 'And everyone thinks the *domina* can do anything. I can't do *this*!'

'You can do this,' he encouraged her. 'And nobody will ever know.' The net wiggled, and there he was, practically on top of her, his feet in the strand below hers, his arms in the one above her. 'Comfy?' he teased.

'Scared,' she replied.

'All right now, love. In lockstep. Up we go. First the right foot, now the left. Good. Try another. First the right foot, and then the left. Open your eyes. How's that?'

'If I had my druthers I think I would druther take the elevator,' she said, her courage somewhat restored. 'They all think I can do *anything*—and by golly I'm beginning to think so myself!'

He stopped directing, and she stopped moving, leaning back against his comforting strength. And a strange thought ran through her mind. Maybe I should marry him! That would teach him a sharp lesson! That's what sister Mattie always said, and look how happy she turned out to be! And when Faith managed to get both eyes open, she was almost at the top.

Mary and O'Malley both leaned over the rail with hands outstretched to help her up the last few feet. The two of them pulled and Harry pushed, and she popped up on to the deck like a cork coming out of a wine bottle. She sat for a few seconds on the deck-plate to catch her breath and then stood up. 'Well,' she said, 'that is certainly not the way I expect Lady Sunny to come aboard. Now then, where is this generator which will not work?'

'Just this way, *domina.*'

The trio followed a rather subdued O'Malley down the hatchway, past three decks to what was obviously an engine-room. Except that this engine-room was immaculate. O'Malley went to stand by a machine. 'This is the generator, Miss Faith.'

'What exactly is the problem with the generator that prevents it from working correctly?'

'This generator,' the seaman said as he put a proud hand on the machine casing, 'works off the auxiliary power plant.'

'And?'

'That don't work, *domina,*' he said mournfully.

'Where is the auxiliary power plant?' Harry said from behind them. 'Maybe I can help.'

Yeah, Faith thought to herself as she followed O'Malley to the auxiliary power plant only a few feet away. And maybe pigs will fly. Calm down. Admit it, at least to yourself, that you are going to need help to get this show on the road. And Harry Holson can do most anything. Can't he?

He certainly *seemed* confident enough. His hands preceded his eyes as he scanned the generator; obviously O'Malley hadn't a clue, and was too embarrassed to admit it.

'You've certainly kept the generator well-polished,' Faith told him. She could see his shoulders square, and the smile return to his face.

'To start, is the button,' he announced, pointing.

Harry reached over her shoulder and pressed the button. The power unit grumbled, but refused to kick over. 'Battery's okay,' Harry announced, and went back to his search. Ten minutes later he threw up his hands.

'I don't know,' he said. 'I'll go back down and get our power people busy on something. We can probably run a cable from the house to the ship. Don't worry, *acushla*.'

'*Acushla*?' Faith asked to his disappearing back.

Mary giggled. 'Sweetheart,' she translated. Faith shrugged and stepped back from the power plant. 'This generator—it needs a man,' Mary said.

'Not necessarily.' Faith's eyes had caught a feeder tube high up under the ceiling of the power-room, hidden in the shadows. A feeder tube that terminated in a pair of meters. A pair of meters whose needles were pinned into a red area marked 'empty'.

Faith walked over to the nearest porthole and watched. In a moment Harry appeared, swinging down the hawser that kept the ship fastened to the dock. I know something you don't know, she thought after him. When she knew he'd left the ship, her smile became beatific. She reached into her pocket for the portable radio phone she carried everywhere with her. With a few quick motions she dialed the number for the estate business office. Robert answered on the first ring.

'Yes, this is *Domina*. I want you to call the oil company for an immediate shipment of two hundred gallons of auxiliary fuel to the *SS Bellerophon*. Yes, immediately. Thank you.'

Mary and O'Malley stared at her. 'There, that should take care of the problem,' she said, and dry-scrubbed her hands together.

'You want I should go and tell Mr Harry his cable isn't needed?' O'Malley asked.

'No.' Faith was thinking quickly. 'I think that Mr Harry wants to help. I don't believe we should deprive him of his moment of glory, do you?' She asked this last question of Mary, who stood and started to grin very widely. Faith was afraid Mary's face was going to split.

'While we're waiting, why don't you show us around the ship, O'Malley? Oh, and I must compliment you on the engines you've been wiping. This engine-room is spotless. You've done a marvelous job.'

He beamed at the compliment and eagerly led them up to the boat deck. 'Master Dicky and milady wanted to have a cabin big enough to entertain in, so they took out lots of walls on this deck. But back here in the stern they left four cabins for overnight people.'

Mary and Faith looked obediently into the four cabins. There were no sheets on the beds and the portholes looked as if there had been curtains at one time, but other than that it all looked spotless. O'Malley was an indefatigable wiper.

He led them to a carved oak double door with brass handles. 'Here is the lounge,' he said proudly as he opened the doors.

The lounge was a large, rather manly room. Here was none of the frills and curlicues milady favored. This cabin had a dark blue rug with large, over-stuffed brown leather chairs and sofas. The furniture had been grouped into several small conversation areas all interspersed with small oak and leather tables ready to hold assorted drinks and canapés. All of the brass in the cabin shone brightly. There was a great deal of brass. The wall sconces, the trim on the oak ceiling fan, the trim on the oak drinks bar and cabinets all gleamed. If this was the way Dicky Goldsmith saw the Navy, Faith thought to herself, no wonder he wanted to be a sailor. I would too!

'This is not too bad,' Mary said thoughtfully, 'but where is the kitchen? We got to feed a lot of people and if the food's not good then the party isn't either.'

'It's called a galley,' O'Malley said indignantly. 'And this ship, she got the best galley in the fleet.'

Faith let that one pass her by and motioned to him to lead them to the galley—best in the fleet or otherwise.

He led them down another flight of stairs. Evidently, Dicky hadn't had time to change these stairs to ramps. Or maybe it wasn't Navy to have ramps in your ship? Anyway——

The galley was enormous. It was almost as large as the kitchen up in Rose Cottage. All six of the stoves and ranges sparkled. The center work island cast the light from the porthole into her eyes brightly enough to blind for a moment. 'Well——' Faith turned to Mary, who was opening cabinets and drawers '—do you think we could manage with this galley for your wedding?'

'It could do,' Mary said with a sly grin at O'Malley's back. 'If not, then we can bring down from the cottage.'

'Okay, you two,' Faith said with laughter as O'Malley turned suddenly, ready to take Mary on in battle over his beloved galley. 'This is perfect; we can hold the wedding here with no problems. Why don't we go upstairs and have a drink?'

'I even have some ice now, *domina*.' O'Malley was still trying to score points for his magnificent ship.

'Good,' Faith said, relieved to see that no blood would be spilt on the deck-plates. 'Aren't you thirsty, Mary?'

'Yes, Miss Faith.' She turned to her fiancé and smiled. 'And the ship, she is perfect for my wedding.'

'Our wedding,' O'Malley insisted as he hugged his future bride and led them up to the lounge.

'Please to be seated, ladies. I have lemonade in the cooler.' From behind the bar counter he brought up a large glass bottle of lemonade and three glasses. He then brought up some ice in an ice-bucket and dropped cubes into each of the glasses. After pouring the drinks he placed them on a brass tray and brought them over to the waiting ladies.

'For this, *acushla*, I can forgive you most anything,' Mary said quietly after taking a big sip of the cold beverage.

He put the tray down on one of the ubiquitous little tables and sat with his own glass. 'Well, Mary,' he said, 'what do you think of my ship now?'

'I think that if we get some power on her, then she be perfect for *my* wedding.'

'We'll have the power,' Faith assured her, 'sometime today, I promise. And then you'll get married and go sailing off into the sunset.'

'Sail?' O'Malley asked anxiously.

'Just a manner of speaking,' Faith told him.

They sat in the relative coolness of the ship for about an hour, talking about the wedding and the arrangements that would be made for the big day. Faith got up and walked over to the landward-side porthole and looked out to see Harry and his men working madly in the hot sun, trying to lay the cable from his construction site to the ship. As she stood there, a British Petroleum tank truck came and parked in front of the ship's auxiliary intake bunker.

'You'd better go down and help load the oil bunker,' Faith told O'Malley. 'Take as much fuel oil as you can squeeze into the tanks.'

'Yes, *domina*,' he said with a magnificent smile. It was that sort of smile Faith was becoming accustomed to. *Domina* can fix anything, no! Except *domina* can't fix *domina*—or Harry Holson, either. And if I were a decent woman I would have told Harry that everything's fixed and he needn't sweat and swear in the tropical sun! she thought. But maybe it's good for him.

The oil-loading was done very quickly. The fuel gurgled as it rose through the pipes and then, to prime the generator, O'Malley used the hand-pump to bring fuel up to the burners, and then he came panting up to the boat deck.

'T'thing is all loaded, *domina*. You want I should——?' And just at that moment Harry came aboard up the hawser line and interrupted everything.

'We'll have the cable down here in about an hour. Don't worry, Mary, you'll have power for your wedding.'

Faith smiled at him, a smile that warned him she had a card up her sleeve. 'That will be lovely, I'm sure. But, in the meanwhile——' And she pushed the button that turned on the generator. The lights came on all over the ship and the two refrigerators behind the bar sputtered and hummed and began making ice. 'In the meantime,' Faith continued with an innocent little smile, 'would you like a cold drink?'

Harry's eyes narrowed as he looked slowly around. 'Done me in again, *domina*?'

'No, not really. It's just that after you left we discovered——'

Harry made another full turn around, as if he was counting the lights and appliances that were now functioning normally.

Faith took a deep breath. If there was a moment when he might blow his top, this would be it. He's a big man, she reminded herself, and he has a big temper, and——

'Why, you little witch,' he said, smiling gently. 'How did you do that?' He came to stand directly in front of her. Faith took another deep breath, stepped back reflexively, and fell into one of the over-stuffed couches on the port side.

'After you left,' she said weakly, 'I noticed the fuel gauges on the auxiliary power plant read empty. So I called Robert in the business office, and he called British Petroleum, and they—— Why are you laughing at me?'

'I'm not laughing at you,' he said. 'I'm laughing at me. LITTLE-GIRL LAWYER SUCKERS BIG ENGINEER!

That would make a big headline for the *Boston Globe*, wouldn't it?'

Faith approached the problem cautiously. 'You're not—angry?'

'Only at myself,' he said.

'Then why are you looking like that?'

He bent over and snatched her up off the couch. 'Because even though I'm not angry it seems to me you owe me something, woman.'

'And you mean to——'

'And I mean to collect at this very minute, counselor.' He swung himself around a couple of times, and her with him. Her skirt flared outward. Her hands came up around his neck with desperation, and she hung on for dear life.

'Let me down,' she sputtered. 'Do you hear me, you overgrown ape? Put me down. Now!'

Mary had given a startled little scream when he had snatched the *domina* up in his arms. As Faith got angry Mary got angrier, and she started to look for a big stick. 'O'Malley,' Mary yelled, 'where is there something to hit him with?'

'I'll go get a shovel,' the seaman was quick to answer. He ran out of the cabin and headed toward the engine-room hatchway.

Harry, still holding Faith closely, brought her up to lip level and gently touched his lips to hers. He caught her in the middle of a mild expletive, with her mouth open. He couldn't have timed it better. His lips sealed her off from the outside world, and his tongue explored her mouth with an intoxicating attack. Faith fought, but too weakly and too late. She gave up the battle, and responded without thought. It wasn't that she couldn't think, but rather that she wouldn't. Once again he had drugged her into a state of passive compliance.

Damn, she thought, before she was carried away. All he has to do is kiss me and I fall over like moist putty. Silly putty! And that was when her mind turned into a four-colored Ferris wheel and went climbing up into the sky without direction. No kiss could last forever; Faith didn't want this one ever to stop. But it did.

He pulled his mouth away reluctantly, and lowered her to where her feet touched the deck. She felt the deck under her feet, but her muscles were unable to support her. To avoid a collapse she threw her arms around his neck again and hung on helplessly.

'You are a smart alec,' Harry said quietly. 'Did anyone ever tell you that? Just a fast-talking, lawyer-type smart alec.'

'And you're a spoilsport,' Faith returned as she got her senses under control once again. 'Have you finished with your Barbarian at the Gate imitation?'

'Not yet,' Harry said as he picked her off the floor once again.

Before he kissed her this time she managed to say, 'Put me down, damn you!'

In a false accent he said, 'I vill ven I yam good and ready, lady.' And then he kissed her again.

O'Malley came up from below decks carrying a coal shovel. 'Here,' he told Mary as he handed it to her. 'I have found the shovel for the coal. It was put away many years ago. We don't use coal no more. You're lucky I could find it.'

'Hit him,' Mary urged. O'Malley swung the shovel back and forth a time or two. 'Aren't you going to hit him?' Mary asked.

'No.' O'Malley was shocked. 'I don't want to hit him. He's just doing what a man does with his woman.' With that said, he tried to give the shovel back to Mary. She didn't take it, but he still held it out to her.

Harry laughed and put Faith down. 'That's right, man. I'm only doing what a man does with his woman. You've got that right, for sure.'

O'Malley was startled by Harry's addition to the conversation. He dropped the shovel on the carpet. Like every other tool on the ship the coal shovel gleamed of polished steel. 'I just got t'shovel 'cause Mary be so upset about you manhandling *domina*. But I see *domina*, she's not upset about it. When he kiss her, she don't scream or moan or such. She just stay still and enjoy!'

Faith had heard enough. It was time to change the subject. It was time to get out of arm's reach. Harry's arms released her reluctantly. Faith, deciding she had quelled the riot, stepped away from Harry in Mary's direction. She stepped away, only to put her foot on the curved surface of the shovel, stumbled, and fell toward the floor. Toward, not to. Before she could land Harry swept her up again and clutched her tightly against his iron muscles. 'Thank you,' Faith muttered, and then winced.

'I beg your pardon?' Harry said, as if he hadn't heard her words.

'I said thank you,' Faith said, just a little louder.

'Could you hear that, Mary?' Harry said.

'Yes,' Mary said quickly and with great emphasis.

'Are you all right?' Harry asked Faith as he saw her wince when she stepped on her right foot.

'I think I may have twisted my ankle,' Faith said, looking longingly at the chair four feet away.

'No need for chairs,' Harry said, intercepting her glance at the furniture, 'not when I can carry you wherever you need to go.'

'Listen,' Faith said, 'I don't need you to carry me anywhere. I can call up to the house and Napoleon will bring down a wheelchair. And probably a doctor, and even a surgeon if I want one. I don't. So please just put me down.'

'Is the gangplank down?' Harry asked.

'Not yet,' came the answer. 'I was waiting for *domina* to tell me to do it.'

'Please put the gangplank down.' Faith was at the end of her tether.

Harry walked over to the couch and gently deposited her on the soft leather seat. 'Just wait here,' he said in her ear. 'I'll be right back after we get the gangplank down and operational.' He left the room with O'Malley; both were whistling up a cheery storm.

Faith, for just a moment, felt lonely. Come on, girl, she told herself with a scowl on her face, get a grip on life. How can you feel lonely just because he walked out the door? She looked up and saw Mary's face. Mary was looking anxious. She had gone to the bar and gotten some ice in a towel for Faith's ankle, which was swelling up nicely. Mary put the towel around her ankle and tucked it in so that it would stay in place.

'Is something wrong, Mary?'

'Not with me, *domina*. I was wondering if something was wrong with you other than with your ankle.'

'Why would you think there was something wrong?' Faith asked.

'Why are you looking so mean and angry?' Mary returned. 'I thought you must be in pain from your injury.'

'Oh,' Faith started with a small laugh, 'I got caught up with my thoughts and they weren't all good thoughts.' She paused for a moment and then gathered her courage to ask, 'How do you feel around O'Malley? Did you always like him?'

'No,' Mary said after a few seconds of thought. 'I didn't like him in the beginning. I thought he was just a ladies' man. An' my family is first-class; his is just shanty. I grew up in a house with water. He was born in a shack with river in back. The first time he got shoes was here, from milady.' She stopped for a minute and then related the most important difference. 'I finished grade eight; he only went to grade three.'

'But, evidently, love overcame these difficulties?'

'It wasn't just love, *domina*,' Mary said with a fond smile. 'My family thought I was marrying beneath me, but O'Malley's aunt, Deirdre, went in my mother's face. Deirdre is a strong woman and she persuaded my mother that O'Malley was the man for me.'

'Thank goodness for Aunt Deirdre, then,' Faith said. If she was going to say anything else it was cut off by the re-entry of Harry. 'The gangplank is down now?'

'Yes, *domina*,' he said with a big, beaming smile. 'An' she's in good shape, too.'

Harry came over and looked at Faith's ankle with the ice-towel on it. 'Is it hurting you?'

'Not that much, but I should go up to the cottage and put some more ice on it. I can just call them to come and get me.'

'Come on,' Harry said as he leaned over and picked her up from the couch. 'I'm here and I can get you to the house sooner than they can. Besides, it looks as if there is a storm brewing. I'd like you to be inside and taken care of as soon as possible.'

Faith had to bend to the logic of his words. 'Thank you for your help and your offer,' she said as graciously as she could.

Harry carried her as if she weighed next to nothing. She knew differently and was impressed by the physical prowess he displayed. They came out of the hatchway on to the main deck. Where there had been lavish sunshine minutes earlier only dark, racing clouds remained. Faith could see the Caribbean boiling just off the reef. The waves were pounding at the hull of the ship.

Something was wrong. It took Faith several minutes to figure it out.

The sea was pounding against the wharf and the ship's hull, and yet the *SS Bellerophon* lay perfectly still at her dock!

CHAPTER NINE

THE noise filled the lounge and the ship. The reggae band, for the dancing after the wedding, was testing the sound response. The portable organ, coaxed by Napoleon himself, was barely making a squeak. He *might* have been playing the 'Wedding March', for all anyone could tell.

'I could blow my whistle,' Chief Inspector Wheeler suggested. Lady Sunny, giggling, put a restraining hand on his arm.

'I believe the duty is mine.' Father Paul, the tall young minister from Trinity Anglican church at Palmetto Point, stood up and marched to the front of the hall. Wedding decorations were everywhere. Ribbons and bells and sketches of the intended, as well as the flags of every infant nation in the Caribbean, added substance and color. Confetti littered the floor, already a week too early for the wedding itself.

The good father wended his way through the confusion to take a position on the step of what would eventually be the altar, bowed his head, and began a prayer. A few people close to him heard, and a small circle of silence engulfed him. The leader of the reggae band caught the motion and stilled the music. Gradually, like a ripple formed when a stone was thrown into a pond, the silence spread. Until only Napoleon, working hard at the organ, failed the test. One of the two boys who were pumping the organ stopped work and whispered to him. 'Whooshed, do you say so?' the butler said, and then only the minister's voice could be heard. And in a moment that stopped as well.

The silence was spattered by a few noisy remarks. 'Dearly Beloved,' the minister said, 'If you don't hush up I'm going to call the Obeah Man!' Instant silence, and then a titter or two. They all knew that the voodoo Obeah Man had no power at all against a gathering of Anglicans. Laughter swept the hall, and then all was quiet again.

The minister looked around the room. 'Is that you, Willie Morgan, pulling your sister's braids?' It was. A loud slap reverberated through the lounge as Willie's mother caught up with him and whispered an apology to the minister. He smiled.

'Mary Grogan. Sean O'Malley. Come you both up beside me. This is the last rehearsal, and you need to see what's going on.'

'Mr Holson—*domina*. It's your job to stand in for the lucky couple during this rehearsal, so they may see things as they ought to be. Now, everybody line up properly, please.' There was a massive shifting of position. The two little flower-girls wandered up and down, lost. One of them began to cry. Lady Sunny took them in hand. Mary had, Faith thought, seen too many royal weddings on television. Her train was at least ten feet long. It was beautiful muted white lace over silk that had a rose design on the fabric. It was exquisite; it was glorious; it was feminine; it was as impractical as all hell.

'Perhaps,' Harry whispered in Faith's ear, 'that train is a trifle too much?'

'It's exactly what she and milady agreed on with the dressmaker,' Faith whispered back.

'Will you demand a long train for our wedding?' Harry asked seriously. 'If you do, you could borrow Mary's. I don't think I want to wait around for that part of your dress.'

'Harry,' Faith said, just a little annoyed, 'will you get off this marriage subject? I'll never marry you! Never. Go away. You're supposed to be at the altar.'

Milady and the inspector walked over to Faith, standing at the back of the lounge, waiting for her cue. 'Well, Inspector,' Faith asked, 'any word on our desperado, Mr Vincent Declaur?'

'The news we have is circumstantial,' Inspector Wheeler said. 'For example, our information network tells us that he has not yet left the island. The lad must be getting desperate for we have several robberies reported on outlying estates. This last one took place out at Lambert's. Only food was taken in every case.'

'Lambert's? That's only about five miles from here,' milady commented.

'Yes,' the inspector said, 'but we're keeping a conspicuous eye out on your estate, especially while Mr Harry is here.'

Yeah, Faith thought, I'd keep an eye out on Rose Cottage while Harry was here, too. Just to make sure he didn't try and run off with milady's silverware.

Father Paul called the assembled group to order and, while Napoleon did his best on the keyboard, Faith and Lady Sunny, who was to give the bride away, came down the aisle together in that semi-stutter step that all wedding parties used. Harry waited for them at the altar, with his father serving as best man beside him.

As the party came slowly down the aisle Father Paul identified all of the participants and gave succinct comment as to their part in the ceremony so that everyone in the hall knew who was doing what to whom. When the bridal stand-ins reached the altar they stopped. Lady Sunny stretched upward to pull back Faith's veil. It was too much of a stretch. Faith bowed low enough so that milady could reach. And then milady passed Faith's hand into Harry's.

The shock of the contact was more than Faith could stand. It's only a rehearsal, she shouted to herself. Only a rehearsal, and I'm not even here!

'Whoa up, woman,' Harry murmured, just under the level of Father Paul's reading of the service. 'Take it easy. We'll get our turn later.'

'The devil we will,' she snarled.

'The devil,' the minister said in his melodious, soft chant, 'has no place in this service. Who has the ring?'

The rehearsal went on. Faith froze in position, refusing to look at Harry. He, on the other hand, kept looking at her, grinning. And finally it was over. The bridal stand-ins turned to walk back up the aisle.

'That's the trouble, right there,' Mary interrupted. 'As soon as I turn to walk back up the aisle the train keeps catching on something, and it becomes unsightly as well as hazardous.'

Mary and milady discussed the problem. 'I think, milady, I need to see someone else wear the train so I can see how it looks and where the problem is,' Mary said.

'A very good idea, my dear,' Lady Sunny agreed. 'Faith, my dear, come over and put the train on. Mary wants to see what her pages will have to do to keep the train in order.'

'Yes, milady,' Faith said. She walked over to Mary, who was detaching the train from her own colorful sundress. The train could be attached to the thin belt Faith was wearing on her skirt set. It was heavier than Faith had thought. 'I think I should put this on at the back of the cabin if you want me to walk with it on,' Faith said. 'It's not only heavy, but it's slippery as well.'

'That's all right, my dear,' milady said. And then she looked around the room and spotted Harry. 'Harry,' she called to him, 'please come over here and help *domina* to the back of the cabin and then walk her back to the altar.'

'For you, milady, anything,' Harry said extravagantly.

'I know that, my dear boy,' milady said with a small smile.

Harry took Mary's arm and guided her back up the highly polished aisle. About halfway up Faith slipped on something and started to fall. Harry grabbed at her arm and steadied her. They came to an unsteady halt.

'It isn't the train,' Harry reported. 'It's the slippery floor. Too much polish or something?'

Faith, half resting in his arms, relaxed and savored the enjoyment. I could get to like this, she thought to herself. If only—— Oh, well, if only pigs could fly we'd have bacon in the trees. What in the world is that thought about? This is just a rehearsal. We are rehearsing for someone else's wedding. I'm just here to wear the train and let Mary know how it looks. He's just here to balance me, in case I trip.

'You must take smaller steps, my dears,' milady instructed as Mary stood at the oak double door. 'And then you bring your back leg forward slowly. Step off with your left foot.'

'Yes, ma'am,' Harry said. 'But the floor?'

'Yes, ma'am,' he says, Faith thought, just as mild as cream. As innocent as a baby. Oh, boy, this man is dangerous. Don't go off into your dream world, Faith Latimore. We two are just a stand-in for Mary and O'Malley's wedding. Just walk down the aisle and maneuver this train for all it's worth; don't fall down, and don't convince yourself that it's *your* wedding!

'I'll see to the floor,' Lady Sunny said. 'It has to have some slippage to it or we won't be able to dance after the service.'

Faith had a very serious look on her face as they approached the altar. Harry leaned over and asked quietly, 'Something wrong? Other than it's not *our* wedding?'

'No,' Faith said just as quietly. 'Shut up! I have to concentrate on the train and how it looks.'

'Of course.'

'Don't get above yourself, boy,' Faith muttered to him. 'I'm just standing in to model the train. And you're here only to help me keep my balance.'

'Yeah.'

By this time, they were standing in front of the minister, before the makeshift altar. Mary, who stood in the back of the cabin, walked forward and joined them at the altar. O'Malley, who had been with some of the men in the band, came over too. Father Paul put them through the ceremony and all the puppets ran through their roles. Faith was nearly in tears. She loved weddings. She wanted her wedding to be as special as this one. She wanted to be marrying a man like Harry—except, of course, without Harry's bad habits. Why couldn't he have been honest? Why couldn't he have been the man of her dreams? It was his lying that caused this lack of trust! Damn it! Why couldn't he have told her the truth in the first place? Why did he make her find out for herself? She came to attention when the minister said, 'You may kiss the bride.' And Harry did so.

Her arms went around his shoulders like homing pigeons and her hands crept up into his hair. Her lips responded without caution and without hesitation. They looked like the ideal bridal couple. They broke apart when the audience started to clap.

'You might seriously think about getting married,' Father Paul said to them. 'It looks as if the chemistry is right. And you look like a couple who could make beautiful children.' More clapping from the audience. He grinned at them. 'And by the way, Trinity Parish is having a wedding special this month. Two weddings for the price of one!'

'I haven't been thinking about getting married,' Faith confessed, 'and I certainly can't see myself getting married to Harry Holson.'

'Marriage,' Lady Sunny said, 'is a very happy state. If two people are as compatible as you two are, they should marry. Not to marry each other would be a waste—almost a sacrilege.' She smiled at them and waited for a response. None came. Milady took a deep breath and went on, 'And you can see how I love weddings!'

'I agree with you, milady,' Harry said, 'and I am trying to convince *domina* to marry me. As soon as possible.'

'Keep working on it, my boy,' Lady Sunny advised as she walked away.

'Great!' Faith snapped at Harry. 'This is just what I need. I don't want milady getting any ideas about my matrimonial status. I like my job as it is. Maybe I prefer spinsterhood. Did you ever think of that? Every old New England family always had a maiden aunt. So stop trying to put ideas into milady's head. Please just leave me alone.'

Faith turned to Mary who still stood there and asked for her help in taking the train off. When that was done she walked proudly to the hatchway and left the ship with as much dignity as she could muster.

Milady walked over to Harry. 'Too much pressure. Too much stress,' she said, and walked out on to the boat deck.

Harry stood there while the crowd filtered by. Too much pressure? he thought. And all my fault!

A beautiful day greeted the real wedding party. The sun shone brightly and reflected a strong blue off the moderate chop of the tide. Everything Mary and Faith had prayed for on this happy day had come true. The groom was on time, with his best man. Both in white tuxedos with brightly colored cummerbunds. The bride's party all looked lovely with their gowns ranging from dark pink for the matron of honor to the lightest pink possible for the flower-girls. All knew their lines, approximately—even the flower girls. Everything they had rehearsed was ready to be done. So far, even Mary's train was cooperating.

The cabin of the ship was crowded with family members and friends. Children played in the narrow spaces between the adults, and were hushed from every direction. The air was filled with the aroma of food baking down in the galley. Somehow it mixed gently with the scent of flowers. Lady Sunny's gardener was still weeping at the swath that had been cut through his flowerbeds.

Napoleon sat at the keyboard of the little pump organ dressed in a nautical dress uniform. Francis, the bartender, sat next to him, reportedly to turn the pages of the music. Faith had some doubts about both of these gentlemen. She wasn't sure Napoleon could read music; he seemed to be playing by ear. Francis, dressed in what looked to be the uniform of a vice-admiral, was already nearly three sheets to the wind. Sitting was probably the only task he could accomplish without falling on his face.

'Doesn't Francis look very nautical?' Harry whispered in Faith's ear while they waited for the bride's party to advance to the altar.

'I'm given to understand,' Faith murmured back, 'that the uniform is one that Master Dicky designed for his crew. The whole staff is quite proud of it. And of his ship, of course.'

'He reminds me of the captain of the *Pinafore*,' Harry said.

'I beg your pardon,' Faith snapped, affronted on Napoleon's account. 'Please don't make fun of him. This is his day of glory as much as Mary's and O'Malley's.'

'I meant no insult,' Harry said, laughing. 'I was thinking about the song the captain sings in *HMS Pinafore* where he polished up the handle of the front door and now he is the ruler of the Queen's Navy. That's all I meant. I certainly wouldn't try to insult anybody. Although I'm not sure that pair would recognize an insult if it came up and bit them.'

'I'm not sure Francis would know if someone did bite him,' Faith said quickly before her mind edited the words.

Father Paul nodded at Napoleon and music swelled from the pump organ. If you listened closely, and if you knew this was a wedding, you *might* have recognized the tune as the 'Bridal March'. If you were unaware of either of those facts, the tune would have remained a mystery.

The big double doors at the end of the cabin opened, and in stepped Mary's bridal party, starting with the flower-girls. The little girls were dressed in pale pink dresses with large darker pink bows tied in the back. They were followed by the maids of honor, all six of them. They wore dresses in a soft shade of rose. Mary came next with Lady Sunny by her side. Milady was dressed in her habitual black, but this time she wore a delicate diamond tiara in her white curls. They stopped for a moment, framed by the door as if posing for a portrait. Faith was willing to bet money on it being Lady Sunny's idea to stand there and be admired.

Mary was a gorgeous bride. The white silk gown covered with lace and lace veil were lovely, but nothing was as lovely as Mary herself. She looked as if she was crossing the River Jordan and coming to the land of promise, the land of milk and honey.

For a moment, Faith felt a stab of jealousy shoot through her. She wanted to have that same feeling that caused Mary to sparkle from head to toe! She wanted to be coming up to an altar where her lover stood. The tears she'd promised herself she wasn't going to cry started to fall quietly.

'I didn't think you were supposed to cry until after the ceremony,' Harry said gently. He put his arm around her and brought out his handkerchief.

'I promised myself,' Faith said into the handkerchief, 'that I wouldn't cry. But look at me! I'm blubbering like a baby. It's all your fault, you know.'

'My fault?'

'I wish you hadn't lied to me. If you hadn't then I could love you as much as Mary loves O'Malley. But you did. And I don't!'

Mary and Lady Sunny were about halfway down the aisle when the double doors in the rear of the lounge suddenly burst open for the second time.

'All right. Everybody put your hands up and no one gets hurt.' The organ wheezed to a stop. The young man holding the sub-machine-gun was certainly Vincent Declaur, but not the well-dressed, happy-go-lucky boy he used to be. Behind him, carrying a machete, was a boy who looked to be about sixteen. And behind the boy was Vincent's girlfriend, still bandaged from her hospital stay, and waving a sort of bread-knife.

'This is a hijacking. If everyone does as he's told things will be all right. If not, then I'm going to blow the bride away. And if that doesn't do it, Lady Sunny is next.' He waved his gun around in a half-circle. The members of the wedding party backed away from him.

All except Harry and the inspector, Faith noted. They know something I don't know. What could it be?

'I want this boat to leave this dock and head out to open water,' Vincent Declaur demanded. 'And I want it done immediately! Or I start firing. Now, who is the captain?'

When no one answered, his eyes looked over the crowd. It was hard to miss Francis with his gold braid and air of seamanship. He still sat at the pump organ and he was smiling a great big smile. A smile that showed his gold teeth. Obviously he had no idea what was going on.

'You,' Vincent said menacingly to the very drunk bartender, 'this is your ship. Get it moving, *now*!'

'Sorry, sir,' Francis said, 'but I can't do that.'

Vincent seemed to be taken aback by this but Faith could see him gather his resolve. Times had not been kind to Vincent Declaur. The spoiled little rich boy had fallen on bad times indeed. Living off the land was, evidently, not something he'd ever had to do before. His clothing was the right stuff but it was torn and filthy. He looked pasty and tired. Faith had read the description in books of eyes so tired they looked like pieces of coal burning in the sockets. Vincent's were like that.

'Think about it, boy,' the bass voice of Inspector Wheeler boomed from the right of the cabin. 'Don't get yourself in any more trouble than you are already in. This is not the way.'

'I can't think of a better way,' Vincent snarled. 'Just keep your mouth shut. You think I can't tell that you're a cop just because you're in mufti?'

'Where did you get that gun, Vincent?' Harry asked casually.

'Back when the revolution was strong, before they got picked up by the cops, the buried it up at Fort Brimstone. I just went back and got it—and the ammunition.' This last part was said with menace. Or what Vincent thought was menacing.

'It looks like a machine-gun that the 1920s gangsters used.' Faith entered into the conversation. Come on, girl, keep him talking and maybe he'll make a mistake, she thought. Join the others and keep his mind off moving this ship. You know damn well that it is never leaving the dock.

'You're right, *domina*,' Inspector Wheeler boomed again. 'It is a tommy-gun. And if that cartridge belt is full it must be very heavy, Mr Declaur.'

'If it gets too heavy then I'll lighten the load by shooting some of you,' Vincent snarled. He was getting angrier by the minute because no one seemed to be afraid of him and his gun—and the ship wasn't moving.

'You can't kill us,' Lady Sunny said from behind Inspector Wheeler. The inspector had pushed her in back of him when Vincent had come into the cabin. 'It's just not done. And it's definitely against the law!'

'Killing us,' Inspector Wheeler interjected, 'is very much against the law.'

'It wouldn't be the first thing I've done that's not legal,' Vincent boasted with bravado. 'Boatman, get out here!' He gestured with the muzzle of the weapon.

Francis made an effort to get up, teetered back and forth for a time, then managed to stagger around the wedding party. He took a stance just behind the bride, on the opposite side of the central corridor from Declaur.

'Good man,' Harry muttered as he urged Faith up closer to the old man.

'Yeah, good,' Faith whispered. 'Good for what?'

Lady Sunny wasn't through with Vincent Declaur. 'Think of what it would do to your parents, Vincent. I know they tried to raise you correctly.'

'My parents never understood me,' Vincent said with a sneer in his voice. 'They didn't understand that I needed money to live.'

'It seems to me you had money,' Harry said. 'You had enough money for your fancy car and all your silk shirts.'

'I had to go and get a job for those necessities,' Vincent said, smirking. 'I got a good job. It pays well.'

'You're living off the weaknesses of others,' Faith said, finally connecting all the bits she knew. 'You're the local drug-smuggler, aren't you?'

'Hey,' Vincent said nonchalantly, 'if others are weak enough to need it, then I'm in the right place to make some profit from it. Isn't that the law of supply and demand?' He looked back at his girlfriend and henchman while they looked back at him grimly. 'Enough of this!' Vincent finally remembered why he was here. 'You, sailor man,' he said, pointing the gun at Francis, 'get this boat out to the open sea——'

'If'n he could, he would,' O'Malley interupted. 'I the seaman, not him. But you can't move the *SS Bellerophon*. An' I couldn't neither.'

'What?' Vincent was getting more and more frustrated. The gun was getting heavier by the minute, Faith thought. It must weigh forty pounds. He wasn't used to any sort of manual labor; as far as he was concerned, that was what servants were for. But he wasn't going to let anyone forget that *he* was in charge. He'd show them all. Vincent started to move quickly to where O'Malley stood. Unfortunately, he didn't look down and therefore didn't see the train lying on the floor. The train was there, slippery as a sheet of ice, spread out to cover every inch of the corridor. He would have to cross the entire area, and there was no doubt that he considered O'Malley to be his primary target. He started off at full speed. About halfway across the veil he slipped. As his legs went out from under him he let go of the tommy-gun to break his fall. The gun went up and then came down gently in Harry Holson's firm hands. O'Malley squealed, 'I got him! I got him!'

Harry reached out to support the bridegroom's wavering stance with his free hand, and barely held him up. Declaur, still skidding on the slippery surface, dived under Mary's little feet. Mary, startled by it all, let out a screech, but when O'Malley reached out to catch her he over-balanced himself and all of his two hundred and eighty pounds landed on top of Declaur. Vincent Declaur closed both eyes tightly and began to mumble.

'I knew something was wrong with this kid,' Francis the bartender yelled as he ran over from the organ. 'He's saying a rosary. He's a Catholic at an Anglican wedding!' At which point Francis wavered too far to the right, and he too collapsed—on top of O'Malley.

'Speaking of weddings,' Lady Sunny said, 'you're holding up a wedding, young lady. Give me that knife.'

'The hell I will,' the girl retorted, clutching even more tightly on to the huge knife.

'I've waited for this for years,' milady said. She wound up her right arm, swung mightily, and girl and knife went clanging into opposite quarters of the lounge.

'Good show,' the inspector said as he came up on line. 'Couldn't have done it better myself. And here come my constables.'

'Just in time,' milady murmured gently. 'Such fun!'

The senior Mr Holson picked the machine-gun up. 'Boy, this is heavy,' he drawled. He looked more closely at the gun. 'Obviously you don't know much about guns, do you, boy? This gun has the safety on and...' he paused while he tried to move the toggle switch '... it appears to be rusted in place. You couldn't fire this piece if the archangel came down to help you!'

Vincent, by this time, was up and held by two constables. He looked as if he was going to cry. His two followers were rounded up by the crowd and brought to stand by him. So many elderly women were shaking their fingers in Vincent's face that he finally broke down and cried. 'The scourge of the Caribbean,' Harry said as the law dragged him away.

'It was such a good plan,' he wailed. 'What went wrong?'

'I told you,' Inspector Wheeler said. 'The whole thing is illegal. *Domina*,' he said to Faith, 'do you have a phone on you?'

'Yes.'

'Please call my police station and report this.'

Faith brought out the phone and after dialing the number she told the police the sorry tale of the attempted hijacking. The mention of the inspector's name brought a polite ho-hum down the wire. But the mention of Lady Sunny brought promise of immediate assistance.

'Can't we get them out of here?' Lady Sunny asked. 'Or at least get them out of the way? We have a wedding to get on with. Let us not be distracted from the happy occasion we're here to observe.'

Father Paul got up from in back of the makeshift altar and cleared his throat. 'If you'll tie them up, I'll start the ceremony.'

The inspector and Harry tied the miscreants with some rope that an attendant brought them. 'Now, you stand here like good little boys and girls and don't interrupt us any more,' Harry instructed, as if they were children. He moved over to stand by Faith, not far from the cluster of desperadoes and local citizenry who guarded them. 'You're going to have to explain something for me,' Harry said to Faith before Father Paul started the wedding.

'What's that?' she responded cautiously.

'Why did O'Malley keep insisting he couldn't move the ship?'

He had spoken louder than he thought because Lady Sunny turned and looked at him. 'He couldn't move the ship because when Dicky found that he was susceptible to seasickness he had the boat permanently docked in a cement casement.'

Someone chuckled and soon enough everyone was laughing. Everyone except Vincent and his cronies. They looked seriously depressed on the whole. It was the laughter of people who had lived through a harrowing experience. It was a wonderful release for them all.

'All of that for nothing,' Mary said through her laughter. 'But I tell you, Sean O'Malley, this will be remembered as the wedding of the year! Even if he did leave footprints on my dress.'

'Mary, girl,' O'Malley said with a big grin, 'I'd have married you anyway. We didn't need all this entertainment before the wedding. *Domina*,' O'Malley said, looking back at Faith, 'you didn't have to provide clowns.'

'But they volunteered,' Faith said, 'and there wasn't any way to gainsay them. They insisted. I'm sorry about the footprints, Mary.'

'It's no problem, *domina*. We just got to get rid of them before the pictures.'

'Perhaps,' Father Paul said, 'you should have a few pictures with the footprints. Just to prove to your children that it really happened. But, in any case, let us start.'

Despite the interruption at the beginning of the ceremony, it was a lovely wedding. It was cheered by laughter and joy both at still being alive and at the presence of love. When the minister said, 'I now pronounce you husband and wife,' the crowd cheered while the bride and groom kissed.

Faith noticed that several policemen had joined the crowd and had quietly surrounded the criminals. They were very professionally moving their prisoners out of the cabin. They left the weapon for Inspector Wheeler.

'Ladies and gentlemen,' Lady Sunny said quietly, but with authority, 'we're going to have the wedding portraits taken now and then we will have the reception. If you all could either move out of the cabin on to the deck or stay over in the back of the room, we would appreciate it.'

Faith noticed that milady never raised her voice, but everyone heard her clearly. The guests started to move and Faith went to the bar to insure that drinks would be available up on the deck.

She moved out into the sunshine. Nathan Holson was sitting over on the port side, on a bench by the railing. She walked over to him. 'Where have you been lately?'

'Hello, my dear,' Nathan said, smiling up at her. 'Why don't you sit down?'

'Did you get your loan?' she asked, coming right to the point.

'Yes,' Nathan said happily, 'we did. But luckily we really didn't need it because our insurance covered the costs nicely.'

'Did you get the loan from Latimore Inc.?'

'Latimore? No,' he said, startled, 'I got a loan from a New York bank, but your father did cosign the note. Why do you ask?'

'Harry showed me a loan paper from Latimore Inc. and when I asked my brother Michael about the loan he said he'd never heard of it.'

'My deal with your father was a gentleman's agreement and I think your brother was overseas somewhere trying to correct some damage from natural disasters.' He stopped to take a sip from his glass. 'Besides, we never did have a loan from your father's company in the purist sense; we merely asked him to cosign the papers.'

Three strikes, Faith told herself, and I'm out. What do I do next? Hide, I suppose, before Harry comes out on deck. Or probe for more information?

'How well do you know my father?' she asked him.

'I've known Bruce Latimore since before you were born,' Nathan said with a big smile on his face. 'And

we've been friends and business rivals for about just as
long. I like him and I think he likes me. I consider him
to be a friend.'

'Good,' Faith said as she leaned over and kissed
Nathan Holson on the cheek. 'I think I'd like to marry
into your family.'

Nathan leaned back with a happy stare of amazement.
'Are you planning to marry Harry?'

'Well,' Faith said soberly, 'there are a couple of "ifs"
to it now. First, I'm not sure he'll ask me again, and
second, do you perhaps have any other son than Harry?
Lord, that's it. I'll get Lady Sunny on my side. You must
keep it a secret until I tell him. I really have to surprise
him. Or break his arm. Or something!'

'I've always wanted a daughter,' Nathan said as he
engulfed her in a big warm hug that made her heart beat
faster. 'Especially a lawyer-type. The way my son is
forever getting in trouble, I need a staff lawyer.'

'Now,' Faith said as she withdrew from the embrace,
'all I have to do is find your son and convince him that
I'm the one for the job.'

'I don't see that you have much competition in the
wedding race,' Nathan said through laughter. 'Just be
firm. He's a very lucky young man.'

'Yeah, just be firm,' she echoed dismally. 'You don't
seem to realize what a big stubborn man he is.'

'He gets it all from his father, girl. There's nothing
to be scared about. He's still down in the lounge. Go
put it to him. Faint heart never won—— I forget the rest
of that.'

'Fair lady.' Faith completed the old saying under her
breath as she edged up out of the seat. 'I don't really
want to go,' she said plaintively.

'But you will go?'

'But I will go.'

Faith managed to squeeze through the crowd at the hatchway, and then got hung up by a group of very large men working their way out to the bar. Somebody must have been carrying a pocket flask during the wedding. The conversation was loud. Interesting but loud. Loud enough to overcome her rabbit complex.

'I've been married for thirty-five years,' Inspector Wheeler boasted. 'Finest thing I ever did.'

'Fools' bait,' Harry Holson returned. 'Why buy a cow when milk is so cheap?'

'Oh, God!' Faith ducked her head, turned, and went with the flow of the crowd, away from the debaters. By careful manipulation she managed to work her way across the crowd on to the starboard side of the ship before the tears really began to flow. The pilot-house on the bridge was empty. Who needed a pilot aboard a ship set in cement? she asked herself, and began to laugh hysterically.

A few minutes later Harry came up to the bridge, rattled the side-door, and walked in. 'Are you hiding?'

'If I am, I'm not doing it very well.' She dabbed at her eyes, but somehow she had lost control of the shut-off valve, and the tears kept coming.

'Is there something wrong?' he asked concernedly.

'No. Nothing wrong. I—I heard you when you said—about the cows and——'

'Oh, God,' he muttered as he held her close. 'The last gasp of an over-age bachelor. I didn't mean a word of it, Faith Latimore. I can't fight my way out of a paper bag without your help. And when that fool pointed the machine gun at you I almost killed him.'

He kissed her, gently, warmly, thoroughly, and then pushed her away an inch or two and grinned down at her.

'Yes,' Faith confessed, 'I've come to the conclusion that I've been going about this love thing all wrong. I'm not going to insist that you marry me. Not right away, that is.'

'That's very noble of you,' Harry said firmly.

Faith said with a singing heart, 'But first I want to apologize to you about some of the unkind remarks I've made about you. I just finished talking to your father and he explained about the loan paper you had. And I know you didn't take the Latimore money, nor Lady Sunny's money.'

'You believe me?' Harry said mildly. 'You will need to trust me when we're married.'

'I know that,' Faith said. 'I trust you—now.' But not very much, her conscience told her. I'll do better. I knew a man who wanted me for my money. And another who drank too much. They made me—skeptical about men in general. But Harry loves me! 'I had reason to be skeptical about men in general,' she told him.

'But not men in particular?'

Faith blushed and nodded.

'In that case, why don't we get married right away? We have all the fixings, and Father Paul is ready.'

'What? Right——?'

'Right now,' he repeated. 'Look, I'm just sweeping you off your feet!'

'Harry! Put me down. You're making a fool out of me.'

'Who? Me?'

'Yes, you. Or somebody. Put me down.'

'Let's first get some of the courting ritual done. Okay?'

'Courting ritual?'

'Yeah,' he drawled, 'let's neck like crazy and possibly develop a reason that we have to get married.'

'I don't understand,' Faith said. And immediately disproved herself. 'It doesn't look that comfortable in here.' His mouth came down on hers.

The kisses were like fire. His mouth roamed from her forehead to the tops of her breasts. His hands wandered everywhere else. Like magic, her dress came unzipped and she was standing in her chemise, tap pants and garters. His eyes were full of her.

Her eyes stared at his chest, which had somehow been stripped. She wasn't sure if she had done it or he had. But it didn't matter, just as long as it happened. Her body was sending signals to her brain, urgent messages having to do with unfulfilled desires and dreams.

'Listen,' Harry said. 'Those deserted cabins in the stern of the ship are empty. Let's go there.'

'How are we going to get down there without everyone seeing us?'

'There's a back way through this cabin.'

He swept her up off her feet again and carried her down the bridge passage to the captain's cabin. It was as if someone had prepared things in advance. There were sheets on the bed and curtains over the big windows. No portholes for the captain, she noticed, and giggled.

'How did all this happen?' she asked. 'Nothing gets done housekeeping-wise around here unless I say.'

'Lady Sunny said,' he told her. 'Any more questions?'

'You mean milady—she's part of this plot?'

'Milady had Napoleon put sheets and curtains in all the cabins. I'm not sure why.' Harry was very innocent; at least, he looked that way.

Faith reached out for him. It had been too long since he'd last held her. That had been about three minutes ago. There was a great deal of exploration yet to be done.

'But——' she interrupted him some twenty minutes later.

He rolled over and tapped her patrician nose. 'But what?'

'But I haven't called my mother, or anybody!'

'Your mother has to view the consummation? C'mon, love!'

'My mother,' she said with great solemnity, 'has to approve *everything* in my family.'

'Well, thank the lord for that,' he commented. 'Since you're marrying into *my* family. Now, where were we?'

CHAPTER TEN

THE guests, for the most part, had left the good ship *Bellerophon* when Faith and Harry were ready to emerge from the cabin. 'We have to find Lady Sunny,' Faith said as she brush-patted her hair, trying to get it back into the style she'd had this morning.

'Why don't you just wear your hair down?'

'Because I had it up this morning,' Faith said patiently.

'So? I like it better down.'

'Well, you may get lucky today. I can't seem to put it up the way it was.'

'I've been very lucky today,' Harry said as he moved up behind her and bent to kiss her neck. 'I love you. You love me. And possibly we now have a reason that we have to get married.'

'Do you want children?' Faith asked as she tilted her head to give him more area to kiss and nuzzle.

He lifted up his head. Faith felt instant dismay at the silence as he studied her in the mirror.

'I want to have children with you. Lots of children.'

'Lots of children?'

'All right, counselor, as many as time and circumstances will permit.'

'That's better,' she said. She wasn't sure if she was answering his question or remarking on the fact that he'd gone back to nuzzling her neck. Either way, she was content.

They came out of the cabin and followed the passageway back to the pilot-house where they found Francis sleeping the sleep of the almost-dead.

'He doesn't look that comfortable,' Faith said as they tried to slip past the recumbent figure in the big captain's chair.

'I'm sure that he doesn't care at this point,' Harry said. 'And if we wake him to move him, he'll probably be loud and sick. Let him wake up on his own.'

'I just think someone should move him to a bed,' Faith said, mildly worried. 'I wonder, does he sleep on the ship?'

'I don't know and frankly, my dear, I don't give a damn.'

'Oh, that's an original line,' Faith said with a giggle in her voice. She hadn't giggled and laughed as much in years. She loved the feeling.

'I didn't want to be accused of plagiarizing some other great romantic scene.'

'Believe me,' she said as they stepped out on to the boat deck, 'no one could ever wrongly identify you. You are unique. One of a kind. And all mine.'

'My dear *domina*,' Harry said very seriously, as if he was making a vow, 'you are the only woman for whom I will play the romantic lead. You have branded my soul and heart. I have no room for anyone else. You fill my world.' He bent to kiss her as a bond to his words.

They moved slowly, arm in arm, toward the hatchway that would take them below deck. They smiled back at the people who were left on the ship, most of them members of the cleaning crew, or staff members from the villa. Those smiled widely at them as they were spotted.

Below deck, milady, Father Paul and Nathan sat in one of the conversation areas. They looked up as Faith and Harry came through the oak doorway. Milady had a particularly satisfied look on her face as they entered.

'We missed you at the reception, my dear,' she said gracefully.

'I regret missing the party, milady. I hope it went as well as planned?'

'Yes, it was a very nice party.' Lady Sunny sounded and looked as if she was waiting for Faith to tell her something else.

Faith was about to do so. 'Milady, I'd like your permission to marry.'

'Wonderful!' Milady nearly bounded out of her seat. The minister sat up straighter and Nathan Holson beamed like a stray strand of sunshine. 'I'm so glad you came to your senses about young Harry. I knew you two were meant for each other. But,' she said after a moment's thought, 'I can't release you until the end of your contract. That should give the lawyers back in London enough time to find a replacement. Although, I must admit, I don't think anyone can take your place. So much happens around you. You've brought life back to Rose Cottage.'

'I understand how you feel, milady,' Harry said as he looked fondly at his true love. 'She certainly brightens my days and she keeps me on my toes. If you don't mind, we can live at the cottage while she works off her contract, and I can work either down at the hotel or at the cottage with your pool and parking garage.'

'That was my intention,' Lady Sunny said as she rose from the chair. 'We must find you another suite. Something bigger. Perhaps you'll just have to make a suite for you to use.'

'If milady would like,' Father Paul started, and then looked to include Harry and Faith, 'we could have the ceremony here and now.'

'What a wonderful idea,' Lady Sunny said gaily.

'Do you want to have a big wedding?' Harry leaned over and asked Faith gently. 'We could wait and have a big ceremony with the traditional wedding-gown and all the trimmings, including your family present.'

'No,' she answered, with the promise of the moon and a lifetime in her eyes, 'I want to get married now, right now, without delay. I do wish my mother could be here, but—— Would you stand with me as my family, milady?'

'I'd be honored, my dear.'

'It would be my pleasure, milady.'

'You flatter me,' milady said.

'Could we have the wedding outside?' Faith asked. 'With the sun and the cool breeze. I think that would be lovely.'

The small group came above deck and moved to the bow of the ship. Some of the cleaning party came with them. Father Paul stood with his back to the sunset and Faith and Harry stood in front of him. Milady stood beside Faith, and Nathan beside his son. And then there was a noise at the gangplank.

The entire wedding party turned to look. Faith gasped. A tiny woman, slim and svelte, was just stepping out on to the deck. She was accompanied by a blonde woman of perhaps twenty-one summers. Behind the two women came a young, healthy man, standing almost six feet seven.

'Are we in trouble?' Harry asked in a murmur.

'I don't know,' Faith returned. 'But she's smiling.'

'She who?'

'The little gray-haired woman in the front. That's my mother. Mary Kate Latimore.'

'And the blonde?'

'Not to worry. That's my sister Hope, the last of the Latimore women.'

'And now the big guy? He looks as if he eats nails for breakfast.'

'He does. That's my little brother Michael. He hates to fly in airplanes. Says his stomach is always upset. If my mother says, Kill him, you're dead.' A pause for reflection, and then, 'But my Dad's not here, so consider yourself lucky.'

'Yeah. Yeah, I will.'

And by then the new party was there by her side. 'Mama.' A casual greeting that might well have been a curtsy.

'Faith. What's going on here?'

'A—wedding. I'm getting married, Ma.'

'Ah. Getting married. We're just in time. And to an Anglican Priest?'

'No. That's Father Paul. I'm going to marry this——' A nudge to get Harry front and center. 'This is Harry. Harry Holson.'

'Harry Holson? Another construction man?'

Two heads nodded. 'Well, your father couldn't come. Bursitis again. I'm afraid we'll have to move out of Massachusetts.' And then, like a whiplash, 'Ever been arrested, young man?'

Harry stuttered. 'I—uh—well, as it happens, yes. Disturbing the peace. Texas Saturday nights get a little bit exciting. Does that disqualify me?'

'Not at all, son. In fact when I married Faith's father he was in gaol. We all had to go bail him out.' Mary Kate stepped forward and attempted to hug Harry, but was a little too short. 'Well, the intention is there,' she said. 'Now, the sun's going down. Let's get this show on the road. Father Paul?'

'Gather around here,' Father Paul said.

'Father,' Harry said, 'I'd like to say my own vows.'

'All right, my son,' the minister said, unsurprised. 'Do you also wish to make your own vows, Miss Faith?'

Faith was surprised by Harry's request. But, she thought, I'm a lawyer; I can think fast on my feet. If he can do it, so can I. 'Yes, Father, I would.'

'Holy Father, we are gathered again today in order to unite in holy matrimony another couple who have found their love for each other. Please grant this couple the years of happiness and faithfulness they deserve. Amen.' At this point the minister looked at Harry and said, 'Go ahead, Mr Holson.'

'I, Henry George Holson, do take thee, Faith Latimore, as my bride. I love you and pledge my love to you for my whole life. Until death do us part. You are my soul, my conscience, my heart and my center. I love you now and I will love you forever. Loving you more each day and promising that I will gladly give my life for you.' He stopped and, while still looking at Faith, he addressed the minister. 'Those are my vows, Father.'

Faith knew it was her turn to say something. Come on, girl, think of something to say. Come up with a miracle. Don't drown in his eyes. But what a wonderful way to disappear from the crowd. 'Harry Holson, I love you. I want to live with you. I want to have your children and bring them up with you by my side. I want to grow old with you. I want to laugh, cry and get angry at you. I want to make up with you and I want to be able to look back without regrets. I love you so much it scares me. But I want to be with you forever. Please marry me!' The last was said as a plea.

'By the power vested in me,' Father Paul continued, although the major parties weren't paying any attention to him, 'I now pronounce you husband and wife. You may kiss the bride.' This was said with a large smile as the couple were already enjoying a heartfelt kiss.

'My dear,' Lady Sunny said when they broke the embrace and Faith had turned to face her. 'It was a lovely wedding. Your mother and I are so proud. In fact, this has been the finest double wedding ever held at Rose Cottage.'

The police inspector, who had not yet gone, asked a quick question. 'How many double weddings have you had at Rose Cottage?'

'Just this one,' Lady Sunny said happily. She came up on tiptoe to kiss Faith gently on the cheek. 'Now, young man,' milady said sternly to Harry, 'you are taking one of my treasures from me. You had best treat her like diamonds. She is very valuable.'

'I know that, milady,' Harry said as he leaned down to kiss Lady Sunny. 'I know exactly how lucky I am. I'm not going to blow it.'

'Good,' milady said majestically. 'Now, if you want to be alone for a honeymoon, I suggest you go back to the captain's cabin you were in earlier and start your married life.' She folded her arm into Harry's, and they started away from the group.

'Let me congratulate you, too,' Harry's father said. 'And welcome to our family.'

'I never met him, but we owe it all to Dicky Goldsmith,' Faith commented.

'You must be kidding,' Nathan Holson said. 'Dicky designed the first pair of shoes. Ever since then it's been Lady Sunny's cool hand and brilliant mind that's made things go, and don't you forget it.'

'Oh, my,' Faith Holson said, another illusion gone.

But then Harry swung her up in his arms, and she didn't give Lady Sunny's deception another thought until Mr and Mrs Harry Holson celebrated their fiftieth wedding anniversary. At which time, sitting at table with her six children and fourteen grandchildren, Faith remembered, and gave a startled squeak.

'She tricked me, Harry Holson,' she told the white-haired man at her side.

'Who?'

'Lady Sunny. She tricked me into marrying you! Were you a part of the deception?'

And Harry Holson, who had learned a lot about marriage in those fifty years, bent down and kissed the tip of her ear. 'Who, me?' he asked. 'Nonsense.'